HAUNTED
HULL

HAUNTED
HULL

Mark Riley

The History Press

I would like to dedicate this book to my mum, Eileen,
who sadly departed during the writing of this book.
A wonderful wife, mum and nanna.

First published 2012

The History Press
The Mill, Brimscombe Port
Stroud, Gloucestershire, GL5 2QG
www.thehistorypress.co.uk

© Mark Riley, 2012

The right of Mark Riley to be identified as the Author
of this work has been asserted in accordance with the
Copyrights, Designs and Patents Act 1988.

British Library Cataloguing in Publication Data.
A catalogue record for this book is available from the British Library.

ISBN 978 0 7524 5997 4

Typesetting and origination by The History Press
Printed in Great Britain

Contents

Acknowledgements

I would like to thank the following people for their support and encouragement throughout the writing of *Haunted Hull*, especially my lovely wife Angela and our children, for without their support this project would not have been possible. Also to all my friends, for their continuing support and help gathering the stories. I would also like to thank Hull Library; the *Hull Daily Mail*; Mark Lindsey; Keith Daddy; Richard Hayton; Reverend Tom Willis, and my good friend Chris Bell, who shared their experiences and supplied some of the stories. A final thank you to The History Press, and in particular Beth Amphlett, who gave me this opportunity.

Introduction

THE city of Hull is steeped in a colourful history. As well as once being home to William Wilberforce, who played a key role in the abolition of slavery, it also became one of the country's major shipping ports; its main trade being the export of wool. The city was involved in the civil wars, and was heavily damaged in the Second World War during the Blitz – Hull was in fact the most bombed city after London. The city is also known for its distinctive white telephone boxes, unlike the red majority across the rest of the country. The city also has another side to it, a history of ghosts and spectres, with spine-chilling tales from haunted pubs and a haunted shopping centre, and featuring the Floating Vicar, Lady in the church, and old mother Riley. These stories are sure to make your blood run cold.

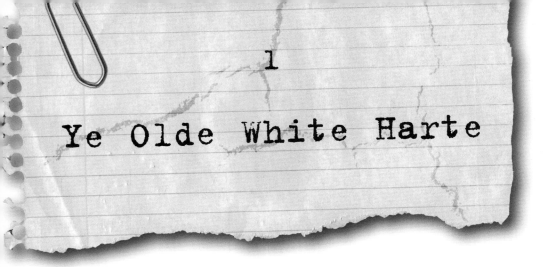

1

Ye Olde White Harte

AFTER hearing that Ye Olde White Harte pub on Silver Street in the old town of Hull was haunted, I contacted the present owners to arrange to meet them and hear their stories. The owners were happy for me to call into the pub, and arranged for me to meet up with a chap called Patrick O'Malley, who has lived at the pub for several years and has experienced more than anyone else at the property. Patrick and I agreed to meet in August 2010, on the appropriate Friday the 13th. Would this date prove unlucky or lucky for us to be discussing ghost stories? Would they even show up to add a little spice to the discussion that was about to take place? Patrick has also written a small book called *A History of Ye Olde White Harte, and things that go bump in the night!!* from which he has given me permission to use some of the information contained within – I thank him very kindly for both.

We met in the main bar area and sat near the big inglenook fireplace that once housed a secret passage (now bricked up but with a small window inside showing where the passage once was). Patrick told me of the first night he stayed in the pub. He slept in a room on the top floor, which he describes as Victorian in style with wood panelling. He told me the room was once used as a meeting room for the freemasons and would once have been filled with fine leather chairs. It was easy to picture a scene in which the rich men of Hull sat in discussions, smoking their large cigars and having a drink of whisky, pushing the bell for service – there are still bell pushes around the room on the walls. Early the next morning Patrick was laying in his bed asleep when, suddenly, he was woken by the sound of footsteps coming from the staircase and hallway. He sat up waiting for someone to enter the room, believing it may have been the landlady, landlord or another member of staff. After several minutes and no one knocking on the bedroom door, he got out of bed and made his way to the staircase outside his room. It was dark and no one could be seen, so he made his way down the stairs, checking each and

The sign above the doorway leading to Ye Olde White Harte.

there at all, and as he jumped back and blinked, the figure disappeared. I was shown the area where this took place and can testify that in the toilets you can clearly hear someone approaching.

A few weeks later Bernard, the then manager, was in his sitting room in the building next door, which was annexed to the pub in 1881, when he caught a glimpse of someone dressed in black standing beside him. As the landlady, Fiona, always wore black he, at first, thought it was her, but looking up he realised it was the same black shrouded figure Patrick had seen in the toilets. However, Bernard has since claimed it was not a ghost as he was tired and that Patrick had put the thought into his mind.

Patrick and Bernard were not the only ones to see the figure. Only a couple of weeks later, a TV repair man was returning a fixed television to the pub, and, as he made his way up the stairs to the landlords' flat, he thanked the person who was standing at the top when they moved out of his way. As he put the TV down he realised that no one was there, which made him wonder who it could have been, so, when he went downstairs, he asked Bernard who it could have been, but Bernard assured the repair man that no one was in or near the flat. When he asked the repair man what exactly he had seen, the repair man answered, 'All I saw was a dark figure'!

A full year passed before the figure was encountered again; this time by a cleaner. Both the lady in question and her husband helped out around the pub, cleaning and getting it ready for opening time. She was trying to light the fire

every door as he went, finding them all locked. He eventually arrived in the bar, thinking that someone must be there, but he was surprised to find the place in complete darkness and the doors locked tight. He decided that it must have been his imagination – his tired mind playing tricks on him – however, his thoughts soon changed as several minutes later he was still awake, fully *compos mentis,* and he could still hear the footsteps.

Patrick's second unusual experience came on a summer's day in July 2005. It was roughly midday and he was in the garden reading the newspaper, when the landlady came out. Putting the newspaper down, he engaged in conversation with her. Noticing that he had ink on his hands from the print of the paper, and that he was wearing white jeans, he excused himself to go and wash his hands in order to acoid getting ink on his trousers. After he had washed and dried his hands he turned and was surprised to see a dark shrouded figure standing in the doorway. As he hadn't heard anyone coming down the hallway to the toilets he was a little surprised to see anyone in the bar, when she became aware of someone standing behind her. Thinking it must have been her husband (as they were the only two in the pub at the time) she started to talk to him, but getting no response she turned to see what he was doing, and much to her surprise, she was shocked to find that it was not her husband at all, but the dark figure.

Entrance to Ye Olde White Harte, via Bowl Alley Lane.

Patrick was eager to learn more about the shrouded figure and began to ask some of the older regulars if any of them had encountered it, but sadly none of them had. That was until a visitor from South Africa called into the pub one evening, he spoke to Patrick and revealed that he originally came from Hull and used to be a regular at Ye Olde White Harte. He said that about fifteen years ago, he had been part of a quiz team belonging to the pub and they regularly met in the room upstairs, which is now the restaurant. One night, two of the team arrived late and as they entered the room they were joined by a third figure, which every member of the quiz team took to have been a monk!

One Christmas, Patrick was given a set of keys to the pub from Bernard as he was going away. Patrick was not living in the pub at the time, but he agreed to keep an eye on the place whilst the owners were away. He called in on Boxing Day to check that everything was okay, and as he did so he heard a loud sigh – similar to the noise one might make as if to say thank heavens someone's finally here. Patrick turned, wondering if he had really heard it, but saw no one. He checked to make sure everything was in order and then left to meet up with some friends in town.

On another occasion, Patrick had seen the landlady off at the train station. Upon his return to the pub he went to his room, and, on reaching it, he heard a 'tut hmm' directly in his ear and he turned, once again wondering what the noise was, only to find that there was no one there. Not long after this second experience, Patrick had been out with some friends and returned late at night and was about to enter his room, when he heard an 'Aha', as if someone was saying 'and where have you been you dirty stop out?' He describes all of the noises he heard as emotional sighs and that each time it sounded like a males voice.

As you enter the pub there is a staircase almost directly in front of you, and it is here that ghostly encounters have been had. On one occasion the landlord was showing a lady who was visiting from Ireland around the pub, and as they made their way up the staircase, just before entering the plotting parlour (a room next to the restaurant) she looked further up the staircase and asked him who the lady was who stood above them; Bernard looked up but saw no one. He told the visiting lady that there was no one there, but she insisted that there was, saying that the lady was wearing a blue dress and looking a little lost. The Blue Lady was seen on another occasion by a man doing some work in the pub. He was sitting in the restaurant shortly before opening time waiting for the landlord to meet him, when he turned and noticed a lady sitting in the small annex room next to the restaurant – this was once a secret room that went behind the staircase in the middle of the pub, and came out through a secret door in the plotting parlour.

The Blue Lady has also been witnessed by a chef. He was sitting in the dining room talking to one of the pub's suppliers; facing the staircase near the plotting parlour, when suddenly he saw what he described as a blue mist floating down the stairs before disappearing behind the plotting parlour door.

While they have never been able to find out exactly who the Blue Lady is, there is one possible explanation as to who she may be. As she appears mostly near the staircase, it could be assumed that she may have died in that area. In 1809, a fire ravaged the pub, and some signs of this can still be seen today in the scorch marks on the beams. At the time, a man by the name of John Clarkson was the landlord and he suffered severe burns during the fire, and tragically his daughter died in the blaze. Is it possible that she could be the Blue Lady so often seen in the area?

Patrick admits that he has only been scared once whilst staying at the pub. One night, he was in charge of locking the pub up once it had closed. He was sitting near the inglenook fireplace finishing his drink before he left, and he could hear what he described as a 'swish' – similar to the sound a sword makes when being swiped through the air. He called out, 'Behave in there and keep the noise down' and made his way to the staircase, but the hairs on the back of his neck stood up. Curiosity getting the better of him he retreated. Thinking that maybe he had left the one arm bandit machine plugged in, he realised that the machine's plug had been pulled out of the wall. It was at this time that he heard the 'swishing' noise again, directly by his ear this time. He was about to run out when he thought better of it, calling out, 'Right, you, it's time you behaved yourself. I'm going to sit down and finish my drink, then I'm leaving,' which he did. After fifteen minutes or so, the noise had gone, and finishing his drink he got up and left. Afterwards, Patrick gave some thought to what may have caused the sounds. Any time the freemasons were present at the pub, they would have placed a young man on guard at the bottom of the stairs, who would have held a sword to stop anyone getting into the meeting upstairs. Maybe the young man became bored at times and practiced his sword skills whilst waiting? If you look at the staircase, you can see cut marks in the banister, which have been made by something sharp, like a sword.

There have been some unusual instances in the pub that have been witnessed by more than one person at a time. One December, roughly around tea time, Patrick and some friends met up for a drink. The pub was not very busy, and Patrick was standing near the hatch at the bar. He was talking to two friends when something caught his eye; a glass on the shelf moved slightly before flying off, clearing the bar and the till before landing on the floor without breaking. This was very unusual because the glasses were on a shelf which had a mesh mat that stops glasses moving when they have been placed there after being washed. The two friends also witnessed this. On another occasion, a loud bang was heard coming from the cellar, which was heard by Patrick, the barmaid and a customer. The barmaid went down to the cellar to investigate and, on her return, explained that an ice bucket had fallen from a shelf. She swore it had been placed securely there earlier by herself and had no reason to fall.

One day, Patrick was stood at the bar when he heard a loud crack. He turned towards the barman, thinking that he had hit the glass fridge with a bottle or something similar. The barman looked at Patrick and asked him what the sound had been. As they looked down at the floor, a large ashtray – one of the big thick black ones – was lyng on the floor, split cleanly in two. Thinking that it had broken because of the temperature of the cleaning water, they picked up the ashtray to find that it was neither hot nor dirty, and they soon realised it was the same ashtray that had been sat on the bar all day.

Patrick started keeping a journal of things that he experienced at the pub. He wrote of another incident which took place on 15 November 2006, around 4 a.m. Both he and a friend had been drinking, and his friend became tired so decided to have a lie down, retiring to the room on the top floor, leaving Patrick where he was in a chair placed to the left of the large inglenook fireplace. Patrick was also tired but decided to stay downstairs; he turned off the lights and took up his chair once again to settle into a nice sleep. Within seconds he heard some creaking noises similar to those made by floorboards and staircases when the temperature in the room changes. This time, however, it was the not the floorboards or the stairs, Patrick knew those sounds, and these were most definitely different; they were accompanied each time by a swishing sound before the creak. As he sat up, he suddenly heard another very distinct sound – the bolt on the door that led to the cellar. He spoke to his friend about the incident the following day, who said that he had heard a crashing sound from the third floor, but had put it down to Patrick bumping into something in the dark.

A few days later, on 19 November, this time at around 4 p.m., a lady who was accompanied by a seven-year-old girl visited the pub and asked to have a look around. The owners asked Patrick to show them around, as he often gave little tours of the pub. He gave his usual talk, describing how entrance to the secret room was once gained, and pointing out the small stained-glass window that was there now to show people where it was. As Patrick opened the window to show them, a chair at the end of the table fell over for no reason at all. Patrick looked at the guests to see what their response was, and while the lady seemed a little shocked, the young girl appeared unsurprised

Another experience that Patrick shared with me was one that took place in June 2007. He and a friend had been in the pub drinking, and the end of the night arrived. His friend called for a taxi and they sat together whilst they waited. Again, it was around 4 a.m. in the morning as they sat there, Patrick on a stool and his friend on a bench, close to the bar. The lights were all switched off except for a few of the wall lights, which were dimly lit. They were in mid-conversation, although Patrick was starting to fall asleep, when he noticed from the corner of his eye that, near to the bar itself, a figure was starting to take form. He tried to ignore it as he thought it was his imagination or his tired eyes playing tricks on him. The figure had started to become more visible, and he began to

see that it was a young man wearing dark clothes and a white shirt, with frilled collars and sleeves. Before he could turn his head to check if it was really there, the figure suddenly came dashing towards him, as if it was heading for the fireplace, and brushing against his back as it passed. Patrick recalls feeling the bump, exactly as you would if someone were to bump into you. He asked his friend if he had seen anything, to which he replied that he had. Patrick asked his friend to describe what he had seen, before revealing what he believed he himself had seen. His friend said it was some kind of strange wispy thing, stating that it went directly behind Patrick and into the fireplace. Although the friend did not see a figure like Patrick had, it had still gone in the same direction in which Patrick had seen it go. The fireplace had been bricked up in 1881, as it once contained a secret passage, which Patrick believed the young man was heading for.

These are not the only ghostly encounters experienced by Patrick at the pub. One night whilst locking up, he took the cash registers upstairs. He was on his way back down from the restaurant when a chap passed him on the stairs wearing a white shirt and dark trousers. He called out to him 'Excuse me,' but the man just disappeared before his very eyes. Another time, he was lying in his bed, this time around 6.50 a.m. It was still dark outside, but he had lain awake for a good half an hour, as the light from the large arch window of the staircase opposite came through the sash window in his room, creating some light. He turned onto his back to get up when, suddenly, a lady

The stained-glass window where the secret passageway once was.

The grand fireplace discovered during renovations at Ye Olde White Harte.

dressed in Victorian clothing walked right through him and his bed.

In the early morning of 11 July 2008, he witnessed a man who was wearing a black cloak and a gold mask, similar to that of the lone ranger; he had black hair that was swept back. He was standing near the fireplace and gave Patrick the impression he was attending a costume ball.

A few months before, in March 2008, in the early hours of the morning, Patrick was sitting at the bar waiting to lock up. It was the end of a shift, and two of the bar staff, both female, were enjoying a drink before leaving for home. They were sat on one of the benches talking to each other, when Patrick became aware of the figure of a woman forming in front of him at the bar. She stood gazing in the direction of the two girls. As she became clearer, he noticed she was dressed in a long black gown, with the sleeves down to the wrists. The arms on the dress looked very tight and she was also wearing a black apron. He also noticed that her arms were hanging downwards but slightly forward, giving him the impression that she was carrying something. The style of clothing she wore was similar to that of landlady's clothing from the late nineteenth to early twentieth century.

Patrick had made a copy of all the landlords' names of Ye Olde White Harte. Checking his copy, he found that there had been very few landladies in charge, but there was one lady, Miss Nellie Nowell, who had been in charge from 1914-1922. This may have been due to the fact that it was wartime and all the men were away in service. Could she

have been the ghostly apparition he saw looking at the girls? If so, it could explain why she did stare, as at that time ladies were not permitted into this pub. In fact, it was not until the 1960s that they were allowed, as Ye Olde White Harte was one of Hull's last pubs to do so.

The final story in this chapter concerns Patricks most recent experience. Around 10 p.m. on 20 February 2010, Patrick was in the room above the Plotting Parlour when he observed the portable air blower rocking on its own accord for several minutes, even though no one was anywhere near it. Then, during the early hours of the following morning, the landlord and landlady – who were on the other side of the building – awoke suddenly when they heard a woman screaming in their room. Incidents similar to this have taken place in that part of the building before. One night when Patrick was asleep in a smaller room there, a chair in the room started to rock back and forth for no reason; this had been witnessed before by a lady who had slept in the same room on an earlier occasion. Another lady once stated that when she had stayed in that room, she felt as though someone had climbed onto the bed and had walked along the bed itself. Another female guest who stayed in the room had removed all her jewellery before retiring for the night. She placed her rings and earrings inside a bracelet, but when she awoke the next morning, she was surprised to find all the items had been removed from within the bracelet and were now placed very neatly around the outside of it.

The room which is alleged to have been the Plotting Parlour.

It would seem that Ye Olde White Harte can lay claim to being not only one of Hull's most haunted pubs, but probably one of the most haunted pubs in the country. So, be aware if you dare visit the premises; you may encounter more spirits than you bargained for. The pub also offers short guided tours around the building with Patrick, who is more than happy to share his experiences with anyone brave enough. On a final, and more light-hearted note, a local group of mediums meet up at the pub from time to time, and one night the group leader rang up, asking Patrick, 'Is anyone there?' (obviously meaning had the other mediums arrived) to which he replied, 'If you don't know the answer to that, then who does?'

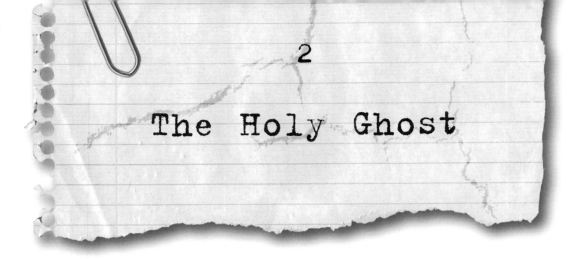

2

The Holy Ghost

HULL was not always the big city that we know it to be today, it was once just a small town. The Old Town of Hull, as it is now know, was once the entirety of Hull. Surrounding the Old Town were several small parishes and townships that have now become part of the city as we know it today. Sculcoates was one of these places. Just over a century ago, this ancient village was about a mile and a half away from the town. The village is so ancient that it is mentioned in the Domesday Book as one of the lordships of Ralph De Mortimer. Although now, in modern days, it is a part of Hull City, it remained a separate parish until around 1835, when it officially became a part of the city; it is here we find ourselves for the next ghost story.

We now focus our attentions on the church of St Paul's. At the time it was Hull's second biggest church, with only Holy Trinity Church being larger. The original church was built in 1847, and was made of huge sandstone pieces. Sadly, being so close to the sea and the salt air, the sandstone started to perish and deteriorate – so much so that if you gently pushed your finger into it, it would go straight through. The church stood for many, many years until it was finally unsafe to be in, which led to it being demolished in 1976 to make way for the more modern church building that stands on the site today. The original church underwent a few changes during its life; its steeple was demolished in 1958, and the church underwent some more alterations before it came to its end. This particular ghost story dates back to at least the early 1990s, during the time the original church stood there. Many people dismiss ghost stories connected with churches, and in all fairness most stories are usually based on myths or legends, and nothing more. This is not the case with the haunting of St Paul's Church; as you may discover when you read the following story about its ghost. I went to meet the Revd Tom Willis to talk to him about the story and about his own belief in ghosts. Tom said that even before he was ordained he had an interest in ghosts, believing they existed even though he had never witnessed one himself.

The newer, more modern St Paul's Church.

It was not long after taking up the position of vicar at St Paul's in 1963 that Revd Willis heard that the church was rumoured to have a resident ghost or two, and on one occasion, as he walked around the outer wall of the church, he saw the chalked words 'there are ghosts in there', which a child had written. Tom dismissed the claims, as many old buildings had such stories connected to them without them having any real validity to them. Soon enough, however, Tom was surprised to learn that several of the congregation had all witnessed a female ghost standing beside him at the alter during communion. He was told that the ghost disappeared into thin air just as he was about to start the prayer of consecration. Tom did not witness the ghost himself and he even doubted those who made

the claims. That is until a friend of the family visited him and his wife in Hull.

The friend was tired after her long journey and explained to the couple she needed an early night. As she was about to make her way to her room, she asked the couple what time she needed to rise for breakfast, Tom replied there was no rush as he would be taking communion at 7 a.m. first, and assured her he would wake her on his return, but the visitor asked Tom to wake her before then as she too wished to be at church for communion.

The following morning, both Tom and his friend went to church and all seemed normal – that was until Tom reached the usual part where he was joined by the ghost. He looked over to where his friend was seated and noticed her strange reaction; it seemed as though her eyes were following someone that was not there. Tom continued with the service, whilst at the same time continually watching his friend's eyes following the invisible person. Once again Tom had seen nothing throughout the whole service. At the 7 a.m. communion a few days later, the friend joined Tom again. During the service Tom noticed, again, that his friend was watching something he could not see, no matter how hard he tried. Tom was, by now, confused and felt it was best to confront his friend once they returned home. After the church service had finished and the two returned home for breakfast, Tom spoke to his guest asking 'You saw the ghost then did you?' The friend sighed in relief and asked Tom if he had seen it too, to which he explained he had not, but told her how he would often watch different members of the congregation as they themselves watched something that appeared to be standing next to him at the altar. He was extremely intrigued as to what it was his friend had actually seen, so he asked her to give him a description of the ghost. His friend was able to give a rather detailed explanation as to what it was she saw, explaining to Tom the ghost was a lady dressed in Victorian clothing; she went on to say that the ghost appeared beside Tom whilst he was standing at the altar before it proceeded to walk away down the aisle.

The big question for Tom now was who exactly this ghostly woman was? And why was she appearing in the church during communion? Tom remembered the stories he had heard of the church ghost; that she may be the wife of a former vicar, and that her grave was to the rear of the older,

abandoned chapel (which had had its ceiling lowered) and the closed off sanctuary, where the original altar would have been. It was now cut off from the church and was awaiting demolition.

Tom spoke to another former vicar of the church, who was able to enlighten him with regards to who she was. He said that there was a grave in the church which belonged to the first vicar's wife and that she was called Hannah Kemp Baily. Tom decided to investigate these claims but could find no grave; however, he did find a plaque on the wall in the area where she was supposedly buried, that had been put up by her husband, who had been a previous vicar of the parish. The story revealed that she had died five years after her husband had taken up the post at the church. Although Tom now knew who the lady was, he felt that he needed to have some more of his questions answered. So, he approached another four former vicars to see if any of them had had any experiences involving the ghost. One of the vicars had served at St Paul's in the 1930s, but he said the whole thing was absolute rubbish. He had heard the stories himself, and believed that they were nothing more than that: just stories. Another former vicar agreed with his colleague. But when Tom spoke to a third vicar, he said that he had always had a feeling something was there and the story of the grave could explain those feelings. When Tom met up with the fourth vicar, who was a former major in the army and had a reputation for being a tough guy, he knew this man would be nobody's fool. He told Tom he had also heard the stories and had dismissed them as absolute rubbish, that is until one day he saw an old lady. He had entered the old vestry, which only had one door for access in and out of the room, and was astonished to find a lady in there. She had her back to the vicar and was rummaging through some drawers. He called out, 'What do you think you are doing?' in his Major-style voice, but as he did so she simply disappeared right before his very eyes. That was not the end of it though, as he saw her several more times in different parts of the church; one time as she made her way through the pews. So, could this ghostly woman be the same one that Tom's friend had witnessed?

Some weeks passed by when Tom remembered he had not marked the place for the Sunday reading the following day. Although it was late – roughly around 11:30 p.m – Tom thought it was best to still go and do so, just in case he forgot to do it the following morning before the service. So he went to the church despite the late hour. He made his way inside, switching on the lights as he went, and stood for a while enjoying the tranquillity of the church. After he had marked the place of reading, a strange feeling came over him all of a sudden. He describes it as though there were 'zigzags' around his body, almost like an electric current running through and around him. He left the altar and made his way into the vestry, where he had been told the story of the woman rummaging through the drawers. He remembers it feeling spooky, but he entered the room nonetheless, apologising for the state of the place, as if he was making his apologies to the ghost. He found himself standing directly above where the body was said to be buried, and once again the 'zigzag' feeling came over him, followed by a feeling that something was about to happen; exactly what, he did not know, just that something would. Suddenly considering what would happen if a passer-by saw the lights on in the church (they would more than likely go in and turn them off, leaving Tom in the vestry), he quickly made another apology, promising that everything would be cleared up soon, then made his way back to the altar. If a passer-by did happen to call in now they could see that he was present. Before leaving to go home he thought about what had just occurred, with the feeling that something had drawn him to the grave.

It wasn't long before Tom hired a cleaner to help out in the church, as he did not want the place to be in a mess again. The cleaner had previously been involved with the occult, which she had openly told Tom, who advised her not to have anything further to do with it, to which she agreed, of course, for fear of losing her job. After some time, she too became aware of the ghost and confided in Tom about seeing her, but she explained to Tom that she had also seen a little man, who she said was a priest. He had appeared to her one day while she was cleaning the Kemp Baily chalice and had smiled at her. Later, she asked Tom not to be angry if she confided something in him; Tom of course agreed and asked what it was she wanted to tell him. She went on to explain that the people next door had invited her to join them in a seance, along with a medium who they had also invited into their home, for they too had a ghost. The medium said she was aware of a little lady called Harriet and that she was polishing something. The cleaner asked Tom if Harriet was the lady who was buried in the old chapel, to which Tom replied no, explaining that her name was Hannah not Harriet. He took the cleaner to where the baptism book was kept, showing her where it stated that Hannah Kemp Baily was the wife of the first vicar. The section where it said baptism had been crossed out and replaced with the word 'burial'. This confirmed to the cleaner that the lady's name was Hannah, and not Harriet as the medium had claimed. Despite this, the two decided to enter the chapel and look at the plaque that was hung on the wall above the triangle on the floor which marked her grave. The room was very dirty and dusty, as no one had been in there to clean it for several years. They realised, on further inspection, that the copper plaque was a little loose and dirty, so they took it down to clean it. As they did so they realised the plaque was made of brass and not copper, and that some of the letters had become a little worn, but even so they could still read the name Hannah very clearly. However, as they continued to clean the plaque they discovered that the name began to look different, and now it did not read Hannah at all, but Harriet instead, much to their surprise and disbelief.

Some time later there was a delivery of new bibles and Tom decided to visit the church late one night to mark out his readings on the new pages for the following the day. The church felt very peaceful as he prepared his new book and he went into the vestry to fetch some water. As he did so he looked down at the marked grave and felt that things were not right, so, once again, he apologised for the mess, promised to make things right and said a blessing before leaving the room. With all the confusion of the names, Tom began to wonder what had gone wrong, as the plaque clearly now read Harriet. But if the plaque was wrong, why on earth did her husband put up with such a mistake? Tom knew that it clearly stated Hannah in the book, which had been written in by the vicar himself. He inspected the floor, which appeared to be the original Victorian one. Even checking the newspapers of the time, the name in them was stated yet again as Hannah Kemp Baily and not Harriet. Something was clearly wrong and this was surely the reason for the ghostly appearances; the ghost was clearly not at rest and was trying to draw attention to the mistake. No matter how hard they tried to understand the cause behind the mistake, there seemed no logical explanation for it. That is until Tom paid a visit to Hull Library, which shed some light on what could have gone wrong. He discovered that sometime in the 1880s a survey was done of Hull's churches; the researcher at the time recorded the vicar's wife as one Hannah Kemp Baily, and also wrote down her date of birth. He also discovered that at the turn of the century the original stone floor had been replaced with a new floor. Tom came to the conclusion that one of two things may have happened; either the new engraver of the plate had misread the name and put down the wrong one, possibly unable to read it correctly

Hannah Kemp's resting place.

due to the amount it had been walked upon by the congregations over the years, or he was simply given the wrong name by someone who had misread the worn away lettering.

Whatever the reason for the mistake, it was rectified when the old church was demolished and the new church erected; the grave was now placed outside, not inside, and Tom insisted the grave be marked correctly, this time with a new plaque, so that the ghostly lady could finally rest in peace. From what we can gather there have been no sightings of her since then, so maybe she has been able to do just that.

In 1998, a sum of £70,000 was raised by the good people of Hull which allowed the decaying church to be demolished. This was by no means enough money to replace it with anything as grand as the original church, but it was enough to build a smaller, more modern one. Once the new church had been built,

the new Reverend asked Tom to take a service there one day, which he was only too happy to do. Afterwards, he asked the small congregation to join him outside at Harriet's grave to say a prayer and a blessing for her. Although Tom is now retired, he still remains a large figure in the city of Hull, and he now works as an exorcist for the Church. He often receives calls from people in Hull requiring his help, including the police force and the local paper. Tom has also had some fame on television when he starred in a documentary called *The Exorcist*, and he also made an appearance on the *Richard and Judy* show.

At the end of the interview, Revd Willis told me that he had never seen a ghost in his life, but there was one occasion when he thought he had. While at St Paul's, he had entered the church late one night. This was during a time when it was still safe to leave doors unlocked – with no concern about burglars – which lots of churches regularly did, so that anyone needing spiritual enlightenment were able to enter and pray to God in peace. He said the lights were out but he noticed a flickering light below the Aumbry (a type of cabinet that you find in the wall of a church or in the sacristy, which was used to store chalices or other vessels, as well as housing the reserved sacrament – the consecrated elements from the Eucharist). He first thought that someone had left the candle below it lit until, that is, he noticed the flame would go out then light again, as well as move up and down. He could make out a silhouette next to the small flame, and he thought to himself, 'Good Lord, I've just seen my first ghost!' His hands shaking with nerves, he reached for the lightswitch and turned it on, only to find to his relief that there was no ghost, just a drunkard with a cigarette lighter trying to find his way around the darkened room.

Ye Olde Black Boy

WHEN I first decided to write this book on Hull and its many haunted properties, I immediately rang my very good friend Chris. Hull born and bred, Chris has a keen interest in its history and has collected many tales of the city over the years. As soon as I spoke to him about the project, he told me to visit Ye Olde Black Boy on High Street, which is situated in the Old Town of Hull. This is the oldest pub in the oldest part of Hull, dating back to 1724. He also said that if I asked anyone in Hull about haunted properties, the majority of people would reply with Ye Olde Black Boy first. After speaking with Chris I found several stories on the internet regarding Ye Olde Black Boy's ghost, and after placing a small advert on the internet I received dozens of testimonials regarding the building.

After contacting the owners, Adam and Helen Scruton, I arranged to go to Ye Olde Black Boy one dinnertime. Whilst interviewing Helen, I was very surprised to find that neither she nor her husband had had any haunting experiences since they took over the year before. How could this be? Adam has worked in several pubs in the town, experiencing paranormal occurrences in all of them, and yet, surprisingly, he and Helen had yet to experience anything of the sort in Ye Olde Black Boy – Adam even worked there for a year previous to buying it.

My initial thought was that maybe the ghosts had left the pub. As a paranormal investigator, I am aware buildings can go through quiet periods where nothing happens for a while, but that usually occurs for weeks, maybe months, not two whole years. Had the stories been invented? Is there any truth behind them at all? Within a short time I soon stopped worrying as the landlady told me they were aware of the stories and could relate them to me. Although she herself had not experienced anything paranormal, she mentioned that plenty of her bar staff and customers had.

Although it is unkown how old the building it is, records show that it has been a public house since 1729, when it was was owned by a William Smith who,

Above *Window to Ye Olde Black Boy on High Street.*

Left *Ye Olde Black Boy from the front.*

it is believed, was responsible for changing the building from a dwelling place into a public house. He bought the property in 1724. There was a building partly on the site way before then – the earliest records show property on the land, or on part of the land, back to 1336 – called Gastryk House, which was owned by a Richard Taverner. It seems it remained a public house until around 1851, when the same address was registered as Scaife, Kelsey & Co., corn and seed merchants. By the year 1855, a Joseph Samuel Ouston was registered at the property, with his trade listed as a wine and spirit merchant and commission agent. It is in 1899 that Ye Olde Black Boy can be found in the trade directory, although now at 151 High Street, not 150. It reverted back to number 150 eventually; however, the date and reason for this change is unknown.

There have been rumours of the pub being linked to the slave trade, with slaves allegedly being kept here after they had been transported into Hull docks. As Hull was not known for being a slave port, this claim has been disputed and it is believed that this story came about due to the pub's name, and the fact that one of its ghosts is rumoured to be a boy who often appears as a black figure. Someone, somewhere, put the stories together, mistaking the description of the black figure as meaning a black boy. The name of the pub in fact links to it being, at one time, a tobacconist shop or snuff seller back in the 1920s, with the sign showing the figure of an Indian Chief. It is said a small Moroccan boy worked there as an errand boy, though nothing as crude as a trapped slave, which some have tried to suggest.

A modern view of High Street.

You only need to look at Hull's history to find it easy to rule out any links to the slave trade.

As there is no evidence or description in regard to the spirit's ethnic origins, it is impossible to be certain whether or not the black figure is the small boy. However, Helen informed me that one day, whilst working behind the bar, a customer approached her and said that their great-grandmother had once owned the pub and a male relative had died upstairs. It may be the ghost of this relative who appears from time to time, and not the young boy who worked here during its time as a tobacconist.

As I sat with Helen at the bar to the rear of the pub, she pointed towards the toilets' door, which is next to the cellar door at the end of the building. Some plans of the building show the toilets to be on the left-hand side, but in reality they are on the right-hand side. She then recalled reports from both customers and cleaners, claiming to have seen a gentleman ghost come out of the toilet door, turn left, and walk straight through the wall into the building next door, which is now student accommodation (although I am not aware of anyone in the building next door seeing the figure appearing through the wall).

A local man called Dave told me that once he and his fiancée were in the pub enjoying a quiet drink when he saw a strangely dressed man walk out of the toilets, walk *through* some people sitting at a nearby table, then disappear through the wall. No one else saw what he did, although one of the men that the ghost had passed through seemed to shiver slightly. Dave says he may not have believed his own eyes if the man had not responded in the way he did.

During a tour of the building, whilst ascending the stairs, Helen told me that there had been tales of people being pushed by an unseen entity. Neither she nor Adam had experienced this, but their dog always appeared nervous on these stairs and also in their flat, two floors up. I noticed that the stairway was very dark and this could easily account for the dog being a little nervous, but then again some say that animals are psychic; this too could explain it's behaviour. It should be noted that not all the people who felt unseen hands pressing into their backs were under the influence.

As we reached the first floor I was shown the bar area, mainly used as a function room, along with another area used as a pool room. It was here that Helen told me one of the funniest claims of a ghost I had heard to date. A medium and ghost hunter was visiting one night, when he said that he was aware of a monkey spirit in the function room! The pub would not be the first place to have such a ghost, the most famous story of this type of animal haunting coming from Carew Castle in Wales. According to local legend, the Lord and his pet ape were murdered in the castle and the pet was thrown into the fire; people today claim to see the ghost ape surrounded by ghostly flames in the remains of the fireplace.

Since my visit to Ye Olde Black Boy, I have heard of another story about a previous landlord who experienced some supernatural phenomena during his days at the pub. A man called John repeated the story to me, which he had heard directly from said landlord. It was late one evening when the landlord's wife was cleaning up and putting away the dirty glasses. As she made her way to one of the tables to collect some more glasses, they suddenly started shaking for no reason. There was no feeling of a vibration running through the building, nor did the table appear to be moving, it was only the glasses that shook. Later that same night the landlord himself experienced something similar. He was behind the bar when he reached up to the shelf to get a few clean glasses down and was startled when a bottle of whisky, which stood on the same shelf, started to shake. Like his wife, he noticed there was no obvious vibration causing this to happen and, furthermore, he noticed that the glasses on the same shelf were not moving at all. Suddenly the bottle shattered, its contents spilling everywhere and shards of glass landing about him.

A few years after this event, when the pub had come under new management, the new owner said goodbye to all the regulars at the end of the night. It was his first night in charge and he was feeling very tired after the long shift. He bolted the front door and then made his way to the rear of the bar in order to switch off the lights. However, before he retired for the night, he took a moment to look around his new pub and thought about re-arranging the place a little. So, he set about moving some tables and chairs, in an attempt to make the room seem tidier. Once satisfied with the new arrangement, he switched off the lights and made his way to bed. The following morning, when he went back into the bar area, he could not believe his eyes, for all the furniture had been returned to its original positions before his alterations. As he stood and looked around he did notice one thing out of place – his pet dog, which was lying under one of the tables cowering in fright. Is it possible that it had witnessed the ghost of a previous owner placing everything back the way they liked it when they were in charge?

Helen was then kind enough to tell me about the strange happenings that take place in the front bar. This is a tale told countless times by people who lay claim to having had the experience themselves. It is said that if you sit in a particular seat near the fireplace, a set of ghostly arms will come out of the wall and wrap around you, giving you a warm cuddle. Many people have heard the story and sat patiently with cameras in hand as they place a friend or volunteer in the seat nearest to the fireplace. They wait and wait to see the hands appear so they can get a clear photograph of the ghost. It would seem, however, that this particular ghost is somewhat camera shy, as it never appears when spectators are posed in place. It only ever happens when no one is watching, or when no one is suspecting anything to happen.

It was on a summer's night when a young man came into the pub, alone, and went to the bar to order a drink. He made his way to an empty seat, situated near the fireplace and placed his drink on the table in front of him, enjoying the quiet. The landlord had not switched on the lights as there was enough light coming in through the windows. The young man sat quietly for a while, until he started to sense someone behind him. Glancing over his shoulder he soon realised it was just a silly fear, probably because the room was not lit well, for there was no way someone could be behind him as he was sat with his back to the wall. The feeling did not go away, but he decided to just enjoy his drink and put the thoughts out of his mind. As he sat there, the feelings became stronger and stronger the more he tried to ignore them. Eventually he could no longer ignore it and turned around to take another look behind him. He got the shock of his life as he did, because out of the wall came a pair of hands followed by arms, up to the elbows, before they disappeared back into the wall. Jumping from his seat he made a quick exit, running out of the pub and along High Street as fast as his feet would carry him. The landlord ran to the door to see what was wrong, but all he saw was the small figure of the young man in the distance. He went back in and looked into the front room to see the man's half-finished drink on the table; he never did see the young man again.

Some people have said that the ghostly hands are nothing to be afraid of. If the young man had not turned to see them coming towards him, then he would probably not have thought that the worst was about to happen – that the arms were going to strangle him, or drag him into the wall. He would have found, as others have done, that these ghostly arms belong to a friendly and loving ghost; he would have found them wrapping around him to give him nothing more than a friendly cuddle. Patrons who have experienced it say that at first it is a shock, but then a relaxed feeling washes over you, and you are left feeling very much unafraid. They also mention that the arms have a lovely warmth to them. The big question is though; do these arms belong to a previous owner of Ye Olde Black Boy, someone who was very friendly and caring? There is the possibility that they belong to one of the women that supplied her trade at the building – it was rumoured that the building was once used as a brothel, maybe it still houses such women in the afterlife, women who earned a living from the warmth of human contact.

There have also been reports from passers-by, who claim to have witnessed a group of ghostly men, who appear to be dragging another away from the pub and down the street towards the harbour. At one time, Hull had press-gangs like most coastal towns and villages did – a press-gang being a group of men who were hired to grab unsuspecting men and take them to enlist into the naval service against their wishes. The men would mostly wear ordinary clothing and snatch drunks leaving the pubs late at night; dragging them down to what was then known as South End. It was here the captain would inspect the victim and decide if he would be set to work aboard the ship or not. Many of the victims were clubbed over the head, rendering them unconscious until the next day, when they would wake up to find themselves surrounded by the ocean. Could this be what people have witnessed being re-enacted outside Ye Olde Black Boy?

Another story involves man who can best be described as looking like a pirate. He would appear near the fireplace, dragging a scruffy bag behind him as he made his way towards the stairs, before completely vanishing into thin air. There were rumours the pub had three tunnels below it, and that these tunnels were used by smugglers, as well as being used by the press-gangs of Hull. Was the pirate-looking man a smuggler dragging his contraband behind him? Rumour has it that one day, when several of the smugglers were in one of the tunnels leading to the pub, they were too busy looking through their loot and managed to lose track of the time, resulting in being caught

The river by High Street, where men would have been dragged by the press-gangs.

out when the tunnels were flooded by the incoming sea. The men were unable to make their exit and they all drowned. Some believe they can still be heard calling out for help when the tide is coming in, and some say that it is these men who are responsible for the shaking of the glasses on the table and the smashing of the whisky bottle mentioned earlier.

A famous medium from a popular TV show once visited Ye Olde Black Boy, and during his visit he claimed there was a ghostly Jack Russell Terrier dog running around the property. If this is true, it could be another explanation for the owner's slightly blind dog being scared on the stairs and in their flat above.

One barmaid said that whilst she was in the process of pulling a pint, she felt the touch of an unseen hand placing itself on top of hers, describing the incident as though someone was showing her what to do. Even though the owners have not witnessed any ghostly happenings first-hand, they do admit to hearing strange noises coming from the bar late at night. They say it often sounds like the tables and chairs are being moved around. This in some way confirms the earlier testimony of a previous landlord, who woke to find that all the furniture he had moved the night before had been put back in its original position.

So, if you are brave enough to visit this pub for a quiet drink, there are a few things you should bear in mind: never re-arrange the furniture; do not, whatever you do, sit by the fireplace with your back to the wall; do not eat a banana whilst you are in the function room; and finally, when you are leaving late at night always leave with a friend or you may become the next victim of the press-gang boys may waiting outside to drag you off to work aboard a ghost ship.

4

Old Mother Riley

I have ventured many times along Paragon Street on my days out around Hull, but with no prior knowledge of the history of the street. I have visited Cooplands Bakery many times whilst there, only to satiate my sweet tooth of course, but never knowing the history of the building it was based in, or that I would be writing about it, and its resident ghost, some years later. Tivoli House, as it is now known (where Cooplands is situated) was once the site of the very popular Tivoli Theatre, which was sadly demolished in 1959 five years after the theatre closed its doors for the last time. In 1954, the theatre had been struggling for its survival and began trading as a cinema, but this venture was sadly short-lived, bringing its life to an end – an unfortunate case for many of the beautiful theatres our country once proudly boasted.

There had been a theatre on the site since 1846. The first was the Queen's Theatre, which was demolished, I believe, in 1870. A second theatre was built on the site in 1872, and was named the Theatre Royal. There is some speculation that another theatre stood on the site in 1815, which was also called the Theatre Royal, but unfortunately I have been unable to find any supporting evidence regarding this, so am unable to say for sure. However, we do know that the site was used as a theatre for at least 108 years. Without a doubt, all the theatres would have been graced by many a good actor, but it is during its days as the Tivoli from which the following ghost story comes.

The ghost is said to be that of Arthur Lucan, the famous music hall and variety star who was best known for his 'drag' character Old Mother Riley. Lucan appeared as Old Mother Riley in theatres and music halls from 1934 until his death in 1954; he died backstage at the Tivoli on 17 May. He also blessed us with the character on screen around 1937. There were a total of sixteen films made about the Irish washerwoman and her daughter Kitty. The part of the daughter was played by Lucan's wife, Kitty McShane.

There are not many who need an introduction to who Arthur Lucan was, or indeed the equally famous Old

Paragon Street, from the 1900s.

Mother Riley, but for those who do not know either, here follows a short history of the actor. Lucan was born Arthur Towle in 1885, in the small village of Sibsey in Lincolnshire, which was within reach of the coastal resort of Skegness and the market town of Boston, where his family moved when Arthur was five years old. Once Arthur left school he started his career on the music hall scene. It was during a tour of Ireland that Arthur met and fell in love with Kitty McShane, and against her parents' wishes – as she was only sixteen years of age and Arthur was twelve years her senior – they married in Dublin in 1913. While in Dublin Arthur changed his name from Towle to Lucan. According to sources, Arthur chose the name after he saw a horse-drawn milk-float with the name 'LUCAN DAIRIES' upon it. It was here they first formed their double act of Old Mother Riley

and Kitty. The pair, under the title 'Lucan and McShane', were so successful with their act that they performed at the London Palladium in 1934. Following their appearance at the Palladium they were offered the deal to make the films, along with a radio series. *The Radio Times* also ran a strip cartoon of the characters.

The duo made a collection of films, however, the sixteenth and final film to be made was made without Kitty, due to the fact that by this time the couple's marriage had broken down. Arthur had gotten into serious financial problems, and was forced into bankruptcy, which he blamed on Kitty's profligate spending. Arthur found himself trying in vain to pay off his creditors by continuing to make stage appearances across the country, until that fateful day in May when he collapsed backstage awaiting his cue to go on stage. There is an old saying in theatres, which is used when things go wrong at the last minute, that no matter what happens 'the show must go on', and go on it did. Arthur's understudy took the lead part for the show, and the audience were totally oblivious to what had happened backstage until after the show, when the sad news about the fate of poor Arthur was broken to all. Lucan, who was loved and adored by many, was buried in Hull's Eastern Cemetery, and it is alleged his grave is the best kept and most visited in Hull; even to this day his fans regularly visit his resting place to lay flowers and pay their respects.

Before its days as Cooplands, the shop – which occupied the site of the former Tivoli Theatre – was called Skeltons Bakery. In Skeltons there was a bronze memorial bust of Lucan, unveiled in 1986, as a tribute to the actor, along with some memorabilia, including posters and programmes from the Tivoli Theatre.

I spoke to a former worker of Skeltons, Mark Lindsay, who was eighteen-years-old when he started his employment with the company, working for them for just over two years. When Mark first started, he heard tales of the alleged ghost of Arthur Lucan from fellow employees, which at first he chose to ignore. Mark recalls that many of the workers disliked going into the cellar, due to the sensation of being watched, and that others had witnessed something, or someone, moving from the corner of their eye. Mark was not overly concerned about this and ventured down the cellar alone on several occasions to retrieve stock. One day, however, whilst he was down

The building that now stands where the Tivoli Theatre once stood.

in the cellar he suddenly felt a presence and sensed that he was not alone down there. He knew none of the other members of staff had followed him, so who was it in there with him? He looked around but could not see who or what it was, and he began to feel a little apprehensive, so he left the room, making his way back to the shop floor. However, this was not the only area of the shop where the paranormal was felt. There was often a cold spot near the doorway to the shop, which Mark later found out was the exact place Arthur collapsed to his death. Since that time Mark has in fact become a paranormal investigator himself, looking into claims like this in order to help others.

Rumours of Arthur's ghost are not only connected to the site of the old Tivoli Theatre. There have been many reports of his ghost appearing at his graveside late at night on the anniversary of his death. Arthur is said to rise from the ground dancing and singing, as he runs around his headstone. The whole episode is very short, lasting for just a few seconds before he returns to his grave, chuckling as he does. Could there be any truth to this story, or is it just a local myth?

We often think that graveyards must be haunted, with all those bodies buried there. Logically speaking though, it could be said that a graveyard is possibly one of the least haunted places to visit – why would anyone visit their own resting place when there are so many other places to go, places which were loved or hold fond memories? Paranormal investigators regularly ask why any self-respecting spirit would visit a place of such great sadness, when they could be visiting loved ones instead? It is possible they really only visit such locations when a loved one is there visiting the grave.

Paranormal investigators often believe that graveyards are not as haunted as people believe, simply because by the time the physical body is laid to rest the person has been dead for at least a week, therefore, the non-physical spirit is not taken there.

Some believe that every graveyard has at least one ghost, a belief dating back long before medieval times. It is suggested that the ghost of the first person to be buried in a graveyard becomes the keeper of that yard for eternity, protecting the other souls resting there from the devil or other evil forces. According to folklore, in certain parts of Yorkshire, when a new graveyard was about to be used for the first time, in order to save a human soul from becoming the guardian, a black dog would be placed in the most northern part of the cemetery, which then undertook the duty of protecting all the souls from evil sources. I have spoken to many folklorists who say the idea came from Sweden, where a lamb would be buried under the altar of a new church for the same purpose; it was then called a Kyrkogrim. In Yorkshire it became known as 'the grim' for short. Two folklorists I spoke to say that 'the grim' could often be seen wandering about the churchyard it was protecting, especially during dark, stormy weather conditions. They also said it was 'the grim' that would toll the bell at midnight prior to a local person's death. Some clergyman even claimed to have seen them looking out from the tower of the church during a funeral, stating that by simply observing 'the grim's' posture at the time they could tell whether the departing soul was destined to go to heaven or hell.

The story of Lucan's ghost leaving his grave to perform another act does sound beyond belief, even to me, although after studying the man and his funny ways, there is a part of me that wouldn't be surprised if it were true. So, curiosity mounting, I decided to go and visit the graveyard where he is buried. The inscription on the headstone reads: Arthur Towle 1885 – 1954. Also known as Arthur Lucan. Old Mother Riley. 'Matches Penny A Box. Stop Me And Strike One. I've Not Sold A Box Of Matches For 12 Months. My Shareholders Are Getting The Wind Up'. Although this is a reflection of the character himself, I have to admit during my lone vigil I saw nothing supernatural, just as I expected. One thing that I did find puzzling, however, was that the headstone looked relatively new and I began to wonder if it had been replaced at some point. More research followed and I soon discovered this stone was not the original, as I had suspected, but one that had been placed there in 2006. Les Dawson, another of the country's finest comedians, discovered Arthur's grave, which at the time was looking a bit neglected, and decided to have it cleaned. The original is still in the graveyard, although in a different location. The inscription read: 'Arthur Lucan, better known and beloved by all children as Old Mother Riley. Don't cry as you pass by, just say a prayer'.

The gravestone of Arthur Lucan, which has now been moved.

The current gravestone of Arthur Lucan.

The building which now houses Arthur Lucan's original headstone.

The area in which the dancing 'ghosts' were seen by a local policeman..

Looking back over the story of Arthur's dancing ghost, it is hard to believe there is any truth to it. There is, however, another possible explanation for this tale and perhaps it is a story that has been adapted from the following; on 9 August 1977, a policeman on patrol near the cemetery claims to have witnessed several people wearing strange attire dancing around in a circle then vanishing into thin air in the playing field on the other side of the fence, not far from Arthur's grave. This was around half past one in the morning. Is it possible that the saw the character of Old Mother Riley meeting up with some fellow theatre performers in the afterlife to continue what they loved to do in their life on earth? Who knows?

5

Hull Citadel

OUR next story takes us to Drypool, which was once a small township on the east side of the River Hull. Its name is derived from 'dried-up pool' as the area is said to have been low-lying ground that was reclaimed from the silt-lands of lower Hull, parts of which remained so wet and unfit during the winter months it was called Summergangs. The village of Frismeck was also close by, but the village disappeared when it was flooded by the waters of the Humber.

This small hamlet was mentioned in the Domesday Book as Dridpol, and owned by Drogo De Bevrere, who was related to William I, though only by marriage. Drogo was granted the land along with the whole of Holderness for his involvement in the Norman Conquest of 1066.

The Humber Estuary formed a channel for vessels from the Rivers Trent in Nottinghamshire, to the Ouse and Aire in the north and west of the county. While this was a good thing it also left Hull vulnerable to raiders, and so defensive measures were taken. A curtain wall and ditch were placed around the township, which was located on the western side of the confluence of the River Hull and the Humber Estuary. The River Hull itself formed its own natural barrier, which was enough to dissuade any would-be attacker. Access, however, was prevented by a heavy chain that was rigged across the mouth of the river into the Humber, both defended and operated by the Chain Tower. The chain was permanently attached to a timber abutment to the east, and any tightening or slacking required for the passage of shipping was done from the Chain Tower. Drypool is located to the east.

Defence fortifications for Hull were granted in 1322, starting that year. The wall and ditch system formed a line of circumvallation to the north, west and southern sides of the town, these survived until the late eighteenth century. In 1440, a charter from Henry VI saw the town become a county, with liberties expanding to Hessle, Ferriby, Swanland, Westella and Anlaby. Drypool remained a parish within Holderness during the reign of Henry VIII, after the King's divorce from

Catherine and England's break from Rome, which led to the Dissolution of the Monasteries in the early 1530s. The reaction that this garnered from the northern Catholics is now known as the Pilgrimage of Grace, although most would say this was a rebellion rather than a pilgrimage, and it wasn't long before the insurrection soon gathered momentum.

We now know that one of the major locations for recruitment was Holderness, just to the east of Hull. Rebels reinforced from York laid siege to the town from 15-20 October 1536, forcing the town to surrender. However, the rebellion was quashed and the leaders all executed as a warning to others. The town was lucky enough to be granted a Royal Pardon.

There was still much support from Catholic sympathizers in France and Rome, who had begun plans to invade England and place her back into the hands of the Catholic Church. King Henry knew the fortifications of the country were too weak and would not be capable of withstanding an attack, especially with the advances of modern artillery, and so Hull, along with twenty-seven other locations, was chosen to be reinforced. News went out to the wealthy merchants of the town, who, at first, felt it was a threat by the King, until he made a promise that both theirs and the town's liberties would not be affected. In 1541, whilst visiting Hull, the King stated that the defences of Hull were still too weak and he commanded 'a bulwark to be made at the Watergate' and what he described as the little round tower on the Holderness side be made bigger, the brick gate at the north end to be walled up and

made into a platform to beat the flank of the town on one side, and the flank of the haven at the other side according to the king's device, also the sluices that controlled drainage around the town were to be 'viewed and new made, that they may serve to drown about the town as the case shall require.'

The position of King's Lieutenant was given to Michael Stanhope, who was housed at the manor house of De La Pole's, now called The King's Manor. Stanhope found the house too large, saying he 'had not enough furniture to fill one small room never mind the rest of the house', so he moved to a smaller house at the end of High Street. It was also Stanhope's and his officers' job to lock the town gates each evening, and to unlock them each dawn. The Mayor and wealthy merchants of the town saw this as an infringement of the town's liberties, forcing them to write to the King in complaint. The King replied with a letter to the Mayor and the people of Hull, asking them to follow his and Stanhope's orders as he (the king) did not intend to interfere with their liberties, that it was for their own benefit, and that he desires them to both lovingly and obediently advance the purpose.

John Rogers was given the privilege of being the designer of the fortifications in Drypool. The plan involved two heavily gunned blockhouses and a central larger blockhouse; all would be linked by a heavy curtain wall and ditch. The design itself was unique; unlike any other in English military architecture, it was neither a fortress like those on the south coast, nor was it a true artillery fort like those of European design. Each block-house was tri-lobed, each 'lobe' was a bastion – a structure that projects out-wards of the main fortification, which meant each one was more than capable of defence from assaulting troops, allowing the defenders to protect either side of the wall as well as each bastion. Each of the roofs were mounted with guns, as well as the first and second floor.

Legend says the stone used to build the fortifications came from Meaux Abbey, which had been recently demolished and had stood just a few miles north of the new fort. It is estimated that there were sixty bricklayers working on the south blockhouse; ten plumbers; twenty masons; twenty carpenters; thirty lime burners; thirty brick-makers; sixty wood-fellers felling timber to make scaffolding; and some 300 labourers. That doesn't include the masons and plumbers hired to strip the stone and lead from Meaux Abbey, or the masons hired to re-shape the stone for re-use at Drypool. The main castle had a slightly different design to the blockhouses, being rectangle-shaped with bastions on the northwest and southeast sides. It was built as a stronger blockhouse than the others, with walls up to 19ft thick and standing in a position halfway between the other blockhouses. The ground floor of the castle had an integral gallery allowing hand-gun ports to provide close quarters defence, sweep-ing over the brick-paved glacis and the surrounding moat.

By the end of 1543, Hull Citadel was completed at a cost of around £23,000. The site covered some fifty acres. It defended the city of Hull for many years

and underwent many changes during this time. In 1851, it was no longer needed as such a big stronghold, and between 1863 and 1865 it was decided most of the buildings were to be taken down.

Part of the site is now The Deep, the world's first submarium; a futuristic aquarium which was opened in March 2002. The Deep is also on part of the old shipyard built by Martin Samuelson, and had become affectionately known to locals as Sammy's Point. Although The Deep occupies part of the site of the citadel, a good part of the original fort still exists today below ground level, and a bastion tower which marks the east point of Hull Citadel is now the only vis-ible part of the remains. It comes as no surprise then that a location with a his-tory such as this has a few ghostly tales, which originate not only from more recent years, but also while the fort was still operational; one being the story of the soldier who would roam the ramparts late in the evening.

The ghostly soldier had been seen sev-eral times and some had attempted to confront him, thinking, at first, that he was an intruder. It was only when the man disappeared that the soldiers realised they had been face-to-face with a mys-terious phantom. Even with the story of the ghost making the rounds, the soldiers knew they still had to be vigilant just in case they mistook a real intruder for the spectral being. One of the soldiers, who was aware of the ghost story, was on duty late in the evening when he was con-fronted by what he believed to be either the ghost or a possible intruder. After his call of 'friend or foe?' was ignored he raised his rifle, taking aim as he had been taught in training, and took a shot at the figure; the bullet going straight through the apparition that stood before him. The figure disappeared before the soldiers eyes and then realisation set in and the soldier became aware that not only was he lucky the figure was not an intruder, but he was very lucky to be alive, as he was facing the ammunition store at the time, which could have easily had a catastrophic end.

I heard a second ghostly tale of the citadel from Keith Daddy, one that I was not aware of before but have since heard several times from different sources. The story, it appears, first came to light in the early nineteenth century after it was featured in the *Hull Advertiser*.

It was said that at the stroke of midnight at one of the sentry boxes, the apparition of a very beautiful young girl would appear. She would stand pointing her finger whilst looking at whichever guard was in that particular box that night. She would then turn to walk away and simply vanish into thin air. This happened so often that many of the men started to refuse guard duty; some of them even deserting their post, but only in that particular box. Not even the fear of having to face the wrath of their seniors could make them stand guard there.

A view of The Deep.

One of the watchtowers of the Hull Citadel.

Only a small handful of men were brave enough to accept the duty until one morning at changeover, the guard was found on the floor, white as a sheet and shaking with fear. The sergeant at arms decided that enough was enough. He contacted the vicar of Drypool, seeking his help, and the two men decided they would both take on sentry duty at the box that very night.

The two men stood at the box, anxiously awaiting the apparition's appearance, and before they knew it the call of '12 o'clock and all is well' echoed around the fort. The men looked at each other then turned to find the ghost standing there staring back at them; exactly as the guards had described, she was incredibly beautiful. The figure pointed, again just as described, and the two men froze with fear, but seconds before she turned to walk away the vicar found the courage to call out to her, 'Who are you, and what do you want?' She made no reply and simply vanished once again into the still of the night. However, the two men quickly realised that she had not vanished, simply that her apparition was being masked by the darkness of the night, so they gave chase. They followed her as she passed the barracks and the ammunition store, before stopping and pointing to the ground in a remote spot. As the two men approached her she continued to look at the ground, before she really did vanish into thin air. The men gazed at each other, realising the girl was not trying to scare the guards or them, but simply trying to bring their attention to this particular spot. But why was she doing this? The vicar believed the spot held all the answers to their questions and told the sergeant to mark the spot and that he should return in the daylight hours to investigate further. The sergeant did as suggested, promising the vicar that he would return later during the daytime.

The next day, the sergeant gathered some of his troops and returned to the marked spot, and ordered his men to start digging. It was not long after they had excavated a few feet of soil, that the men found the decaying remains of a young woman. The corpse was taken to the infirmary, where a doctor was waiting after being summoned by a soldier. The doctor inspected the body closely, telling the sergeant they were the remains of a female, between twenty and twenty-three years of age. She had been murdered and buried for at least twelve months or more. The furious sergeant knew that one of the soldiers must have been responsible and demanded an investigation take place immediately. The soldiers were informed and one soldier, deciding that he did not wish to wait until he was called upon, made his way to the sergeant's room, where he made a full confession. He had murdered the young girl, who was from Drypool,

roughly about a year ago whilst drunk one evening. Fearing his punishment he had buried her in the grounds of the fort. The soldier was taken to his hometown of Glasgow to stand trial for the crime, being sentenced to hang for his crime and for his silence. After the trial the ghost was never seen again and the soldiers were no longer afraid to resume duty at the box.

In 2008, a ghost story accompanied by a photograph appeared in the national papers about The Deep. A 21-year-old dentistry student called Emma, from Doncaster, believed she had caught a disembodied ghostly head on the camera of her mobile phone. The ghostly image was not seen at the time the photo was taken, and it was only when Emma returned home and glanced through the pictures with her boyfriend that the image was first seen. Her boyfriend asked her, 'What is that?' as he pointed at the picture, to which she replied, 'It's a shark.' 'No, the face,' he said. The pair were shocked as they examined it more closely. Emma was accompanied by her father, Alan, at the time the photo was taken, and as there was no one else present in the glass tunnel at The Deep, people speculated that the image must be her father's reflection. This was quickly denied by Emma, who said the image bared no resemblance to her dad.

People soon began to speculate that there was a paranormal reason for the face. Bosses at The Deep confirmed that the pair were the only ones present in the tunnel at the time, after scouring through hours of CCTV footage taken of the tunnel. An executive at The Deep said:

We are a Scientific Centre and we're sure there must be a logical explanation. It's just we cannot find it. There has to be some sort of optical illusion or a possible reflection of images between the window, but we cannot figure out how it has been done.

Not satisfied, staff took things a little further, trying to recreate the conditions in the tunnel in an attempt to see if a reflection could appear, but all of this was to no avail. Finally, a parapsychologist suggested the only other explanation could be that it was some sort of thought form projected into the image. Many people accept this explanation, while others argue that such a feat is impossible. But, in 1964, a man called Ted Serios claimed it was possible to actually photograph a person's thoughts; calling it Thoughtography. Serios claimed that he could perform this and underwent some tests under the guidance of Dr Julie Eisenbud. He took a camera (a Polaroid), pointed it towards himself, and took photos. He got lots of pictures of himself, obviously, although some appeared as blacked-out prints. He had also produced some printed scenes from London, which included images of Westminster Abbey, and the canals in Venice. For many sceptical people the explanation was fraud; allegedly Ted was once caught sneaking a small marble with a photograph on it into the little tube attached to the front of the camera he used. However, there had been occasions where he did achieve some success whilst performing under strict conditions, so maybe the parapsychologist's explanation may not be as crazy as some would think.

The site of the aquarium is situated on the site of an old isolation hospital, which had once housed smallpox victims. Also, in the immediate vicinity there once stood a blockhouse, associated with a notorious history of ghastly torture and, in many cases, death.

A local story tells of a man who tried to escape the blockhouse but caught his neck on the iron bars of his cell. He was seriously wounded during the incident but this did not deter him and he managed to make it a short way along the River Hull, before dropping dead on the bank. Some people came forward during the 1970s and '80s, claiming to have both seen and heard him running along the banks of the river. If it is that The Deep was built on the spot where this fellow met his untimely death, is it possible that it was his disembodied head appearing in Emma's picture? One local I spoke to also said that a night-watchman claims to have spotted what he called a shadowy figure at around the same time, and in the same area. Although there have been no further reports of activity on the site, not to my knowledge anyhow, it may just well be that The Deep has more stories to reveal to us in the future. One thing I am sure of, though, is that I will be listening out for them.

6

The Hull Prison Ghost

THERE is an old saying when it comes to getting married; the words 'I will' are the shortest sentence, and the words 'I do' are the longest sentence. Although many marriages are happy and strong relationships, unfortunately, this is not the case for all marriages; in some instances the marriage is very much like that of an old house – underneath the perfect exterior there are cracks in the walls, cracks that are not always visible, even to those closest to the people in question. Sometimes these relationships eventually break down, leading to a long and sometimes bitter divorce, but from time to time they result in an untimely end, such as murder. This is the case with our next story, which involves a couple named Ethel and Arthur Major, whose relationship appeared to all those who knew them to be a happy and strong one, however, this was not the case. We often hear tales of husbands who have killed their wives; however, we find the roles reversed in this tale, as the murderer happens to be the wife and the victim her husband.

There has been numerous research conducted into the minds of murderers, in the hope of finding an answer to what motivates people to kill. After years of research it is said, statistically, that most murders are committed by men. In fact, it is said that the amount of murders committed by men is 93 per cent. People sometimes believe that women are incapable of committing such heinous acts as they are often viewed as being more gentile and caring in their nature. Scientists have studied these facts in search for answers as to why the percentage is so high in males, and yet so low in females. They have come to the conclusion that males have much smaller orbital frontal regions, part of which is the amygdale – an almond like shaped set of neurons located deep within the medial temporal lobe of the brain. Its function is to deal with emotions, fear and pleasures. Therefore, due to this being substantially smaller, scientists believe that men are unable to deal with emotions as women do. But, despite all the statistics, some murders are just crimes of passion or jealousy and nothing more.

Arthur Major worked as a lorry driver and farm worker, and most people thought him a hardworking man. He had fought, and been injured, in the First World War. He married a lady called Ethel Lillie Brown, the daughter of a Lincolnshire gamekeeper and they had a son together, who they called Lawrence. Unbeknownst to her husband, this was not Ethel's first child; her four-year-old 'sister' Auriel was really her illegitimate child. She managed to keep this secret from her husband for around ten years, until the couple, along with their son, moved out of Ethel's parents' home in 1929, to a home of their own in Kirkby-on-Bain. Not long after settling into their new house, Arthur was told by some village gossips that Auriel was actually Ethel's child, who she had given birth to at the age of twenty-four. Once the secret was revealed to Arthur, he became furious with his wife, resulting in the once happy marriage turning into one of hatred and despise. When Ethel refused to tell Arthur the name of Auriel's father, he became increasingly angry and violent towards his wife, drinking heavily and constantly rowing with her, resulting in both of their lives becoming miserable. The marriage was to suffer another setback some five years later, when Ethel discovered love letters to her husband from a woman called Rose. Ethel went to see Rose's husband, Joseph, to tell him about the letters his wife had sent her husband and that claimed she was having an affair with him, but Joseph refused to believe her.

As the old adage goes, there is nothing worse than a woman scorned, and scorned Ethel most certainly was. She told everyone and anyone who would listen about her cheating spouse. She even went to the council from whom they rented their marital home and tried to have him evicted. She went to the police station, telling them that Arthur was always drunk, and when they would not listen she told them he was even drunk when driving. She then went on to tell them that he was a violent man. Arthur retaliated by informing everyone that he would not be held accountable for his wife's debts and she could go to prison for them. Eventually, Ethel confronted Arthur, asking him what he was going to do about the love letters, to which he replied he would do nothing and even suggested to her that she do something about it herself.; a suggestion that, maybe, he should have kept to himself for if he had he may have lived a little longer and Ethel may not have made her way to the gallows.

Many believe the outburst by Arthur could very well have been what drove Ethel to murder him on 22 May 1934. Not long afterwards, Arthur became very ill, so ill he was kept to his bed, unable to get up, and he complained of being in pain. His wife called for the family doctor, explaining that Arthur had only started complaining of the pain after he had eaten some corned beef. The doctor did not believe it was food poisoning, and instead diagnosed Arthur as having epileptic fits. Arthur died just two days after and his doctor signed the cause of death on his death certificate as *Status Epilepticus* – meaning his brain was suffering from persistent seizures. Ethel, only too happy to accept the ruling, insisted that her husband was buried straight away and proceeded with arrangements for his funeral on the following Sunday. A neighbour became suspicious and wrote to the coroner's office regarding the subject, claiming that a black and white dog, which had eaten scraps of corned beef from Arthur's plate, had died the next day. The coroner had the dog exhumed and ran some tests. The dog's body was found to contain strychnine; twelve grains in total. The funeral was immediately postponed in order for a post-mortem to be carried out. To the surprise of many, his body was found to contain 127 grains of strychnine — the actual cause of death. When the police searched Ethel's council home, they found a hidden suitcase that contained some clothes and a purse. Upon opening the purse they saw some scrunched up paper with the words 'mother's penny' written on it. Curious as to what this meant they opened it, to find a penny and a worn-down key. They discovered later that the key fitted a box kept at her father's house, which contained the poison used to kill her husband. Even then Ethel denied any knowledge of the box or its contents; sadly for Ethel her father confirmed otherwise.

Consequently, Ethel was arrested for the murder, and her trial was held at the Lincolnshire assizes in the November of 1934. During the trial, the family doctor told the court that Ethel had once said to him, after discovering her husband's affair, 'Now you see why it is I have been ill. A man like him is not fit to live. I will do him in.' The doctor informed the court that he did not take her seriously and never believed for a minute that she meant it. However, more evidence was brought before the Bench. During questioning, Ethel told one of the detectives that she 'never had any strychnine poison', to which the detective replied, 'I have never mentioned strychnine, and how did you know your husband died of strychnine poisoning?' Ethel replied, 'I must have made a mistake then.' Although her defence claimed that her solicitor had told her about the strychnine, Ethel's own admission to it being her mistake was enough to find her guilty of the murder. The jury found her guilty, but they recommended to the court that mercy should be shown. Ethel was sent to Hull Prison, where, on 19 December 1934, she was hanged. The people of Hull had petitioned against the hanging and held out for a reprieve.

While in Hull Prison, the date of her execution nearing, the Governer, Mr Roberts, was concerned with Ethel's behaviour and ordered that she be removed from her room above the hospital ward the night before her execution and taken to the condemned cell on the men's wing. She would be escorted by two female officers, along with the Matron, who would stay with her that night. However, as Ethel was so distraught and anxious, the job of taking her to the scaffold was to be performed by a male officer. Sister O'Gara would relieve Matron and help the medical officer deal with the preparation before the hanging; she would also prepare the body afterwards for the coroner. Reverend Fraser was responsible for the spiritual side of things, and the burial, which took place

Hull Prison.

at 2 p.m. The coroner listed the death as a dislocated vertebrae, Ethel was only 4ft 11½in and weighed just 123lbs.

On the day of the hanging a large crowd gathered outside the prison, looking at the clock above the entrance and waiting for someone to come out with the news that a reprieve was given, but it never was.

The first prisoner to be hanged at Hull was Arthur Richardson in 1902, and, over a thirty-two-year period, ten more people were hanged at the prison; Ethel being one of them. She was the only woman ever hanged at Hull and she was the last person to be hanged at the prison; her hangman was the infamous Tom Pierrepoint and his assistant – his nephew Albert Pierrepoint, who would eventually become more famous than him. Ethel was lucky enough to have been hanged within the prison walls unlike some others, such as Frances Kidder, who was the last woman to be hanged in public on 2 April 1868; the same year the passing of the Capital Punishment Act ruled that all hangings had to take place within the prison walls from then on. History shows us that between 1868 and 1955 a total of forty-one women were hanged inside the walls of prisons in Britain. Then followed the Murder (Abolition of Death Penalty) Act of 1965; passed on 8 November that year, which replaced the penalty of death with a mandatory sentence of life imprisonment, as many now felt that hanging was an inhumane act itself, and not the deterrent everyone once believed it was.

The Pierrepoint family became the most notorious hangmen in the UK and it all began with Tom's younger brother, Henry. Henry was the first to become a hangman in 1901; a career that lasted just ten years. It was rumoured he had problems dealing with the psychological side of things, causing him to drink heavily, and he was eventually sacked. After turning up at a prison in Essex drunk, his apprentice had to perform the deed after a fight broke out between the two and the next day the apprentice wrote to the Home Office and informed them about Henry's behaviour, resulting in his dismissal. Henry's son, Albert, was to become Britain's most well-known and prolific hangmen, in a career that lasted from 1932 to 1956. Albert is believed to have hanged 435 people in that time, including seventeen women, as well as the infamous John George Haigh, who was dubbed 'The Acid Bath Murderer' in the 1940s; John Reginald Halliday Christie, a serial killer who was active during the 1940s and '50s; Derek Bentley, aged nineteen, was hanged for murder in what is still one of the country's most controversial cases in British legal history. He also hanged Ruth Ellis who, on 13 July 1955, at the age of twenty-eight, was the last woman ever hanged in the UK at London's Holloway Prison.

Going back to our story, however, it was Albert's uncle Tom who had the responsibility for hanging Ethel. Tom, Henry's older brother, had been convinced to apply to become a hangman's apprentice in 1906, which he did, assisting his brother before becoming one of the best hangmen in the country until his retirement in 1946, when he was in is seventies. No one knows exactly how many people he hanged in a career that lasted nearly four decades, but it is estimated to being just short of 300.

Hull Prison was opened in 1870 and held both men and women. It is steeped in history and was even used as a military prison in 1939. In 1950 the prison re-opened and, in 1969, it underwent extensive security work to become one of the country's first maximum security prisons. It is often described as a typical Victorian-style prison. It suffered serious damage in 1976 during a three-day riot by inmates. Protesting prisoners went on a rampage, destroying their cells, smashing furniture up and breaking doors, before climbing onto the roof of the prison, where they hurled roof slates at passers-by, including the firemen who had been called in to attend the fires which some prisoners had started, resulting in two thirds of the prison being destroyed. In 1986, HMP Hull became a local remand prison and, in 2002, the prison underwent a large expansion, which included four new wings.

I have now heard from several people who all believe that the prison was subject to poltergeist activity after the expansion was completed.

The prison on Hedon Road is not Hull's first prison either. After speaking to staff at a local museum, I discovered that the town's first prison was believed to be near the Guildhall in 1299; along Waverley Street and Great Thornton Street there was a gallows; a house of correction in Market Place in 1620; a female prison on Anlaby Road, and, in 1785, a gaol was built on Castle Street.

Since Ethel's death there have been rumours of both prisoners and wardens alike allegedly witnessing her ghost wandering the prison grounds. She has been seen directly over the spot where her execution took place, as well as near the area she was incarcerated prior to the hanging. I spoke to a retired police officer, Tony, who had a relative that had worked at the prison. Tony was told by his relative that during his time at the prison he witnessed Ethel, but only ever on one occasion. It was nearing the end of his shift when he saw her; the meeting was very brief but it was long enough for him to get a good look at her and to see that she fitted the description of Ethel Major. At first he thought it was due to tiredness and his mind playing tricks on him, that was until he overheard several other wardens speaking to one another about their own experiences regarding Ethel. They each described the little lady as having a charming smile, she never spoke or appeared in a menacing manner to anyone, she just smiled before wandering off; this was the exact same experience Tony's relative had had during his own encounter.

As some of the sightings are nearly three quarters of a century old, it is impossible to verify the authenticity of any of these tales. I wondered if Ethel's ghost is ever seen to this day, and after making contact with the prison, I was invited to meet with Rob Nicholson, an officer and the man behind the exhibition room on-site, to see if there was any truth to the ghostly goings-on at the prison, or if he himself had had any experiences during his days at the prison. It proved to be a worthwhile meeting. Rob joined Hull Prison in 1991 and had been working there for a couple of years before he had his experience, in either 1994 or 1995, whilst working on C wing. Unbeknownst to Rob at the time, that particular wing used to be where they kept female prisoners. Rob was working the nightshift and his duties involved lock-down – making sure all the prisoners were in their cells and that the doors were securely locked. Later on, he was performing his duties and checking that all the prisoners were in their beds. In order to do this he had to look through the viewing section of the cell doors, which was a 2-inch thick pane of glass. He made his way upstairs to what they call the Two's Floor, and, as he reached a recess in the wall, a bread roll came flying out of said recess, hitting a cell door opposite before falling to the floor and rolling away. Due to the obvious dangers, Rob did not go into the darkened area to apprehend the person responsible. Thinking that a prisoner was loose, he made his way to a safe area and reported a full-scale alert. The area was searched thoroughly and, much to his and everyone else's surprise, all the prisoners were found to be safely locked up; yet the bread roll was still on the floor where it had landed. Rob believes that the only explanation for the incident is that it must have been a ghost; although he would have preferred it to be a loose prisoner. The bread roll was thrown with some force and Rob assumed that it had been thrown by a male. It was only years later, when Rob was gathering information on the prison in order to open to the 'within these walls' exhibition on site, that he discovered the story of Ethel's ghost and that C wing had been the female wing of the prison where Ethel would have stayed. Rob said he could only liken the fear he had felt to an occasion where he and some fellow officers had found a prisoner who had hanged himself and they had to cut him down.

Another tale concerns a prisoner from out of town who was brought in and placed on B wing. He knew nothing of the area and had not been at the prison long enough to have heard any of the ghost stories, however, during the night he pressed the distress button in his cell and, when the guards arrived to see what was wrong, he complained of a bespectacled woman being in there wih him. The same thing happened the following night so he was moved to another empty cell on the same level, but once again the young man pressed his distress button, claiming the woman had appeared to him again. To save any further night time calls, the prisoner was moved to another wing and he never saw her again. Ethel Major wore spectacles.

Another tale involves a guard who had an experience with Ethel that was scared him so, he froze on the spot. The story was related to Rob by one of the dog handlers at the prison, who said that he had entered one of the wings to find a fellow warden hanging on to a handrail, as white as snow. He asked what was wrong but received no reply and so he decided it was best to move the warden away from the area; he literally had to pry his hands off the rail and escort him out. Once away from the area he asked the officer what was wrong, and the man replied that as he was walking passed the cells he felt the tail of his tunic raise (this was when the uniforms were the type seen in the hit TV series *Porridge*) and he heard a softly spoken female voice say, 'Go on naughty boy'. At this time, the prison was an all-male prison.

Rob told me me that the gallows used to be situated in an area now used by the gardener, and that guards have observed the prison dogs lowering their heads as they pass by; it is said that canines can smell the scene of a death even years after the event. The dogs, which are Alsatians, also behave in a strange way when they are near the reception area of the prison. The handlers have observed one of the dogs standing to attention, snarling and growling, and baring its teeth, as if in a confrontational situation, even when there is no one there. Rob discovered that that particular area was once used as the female exercise yard. Does Ethel's ghost or possibly another female spirit still linger there?

With all this information I asked myself again if I believed there was any truth to the stories of Ethel haunting the prison. Looking at the evidence, the several stories I have recently been informed of, told to me by a man who has nothing to gain from lying, and the fact that these stories have never been told publicly before, then I am more inclined to say that these claims are true. There have been many instances where too much publicity has been sought, begging the reliability and validity behind the stories, which causes many to think they are fabricated tales and nothing more. From the start of my research into Hull Prison, something has been telling me — some sort of gut instinct — that these claims of Ethel's ghost haunting the prison are true. This is often the case with true ghost sightings; some tales are honest while some are fabricated. One thing I can say is that Rob's own personal story has left its mark in his mind, and I left the building with no doubts that his experience was genuine.

7

The Floating Vicar

FROM time to time you hear a story about a haunting that appears to originate more from myth than truth. Sometimes, however, there is an element of truth to the tale but it has been adapted, with names and dates being added, in an attempt to create validity to the original tale. This usually occurs when someone feels they may not be believed when they claim to have witnessed a ghost. This may well be the case with the story of Reverend Yates, who, it is said, was the vicar from St Mary's on Lowgate, and who alleg-edly haunts the old grammar school on Trinity Square. People believe they have seen him 'floating' along the first floor corridor of the building, and there are many passers-by who say they have seen him through the window. There appear to be several witnesses who all tell the same story about the figure, who appears to be dressed in clothing similar to a vicar of the late nineteenth century. It is said that if you do witness him, it may mean instant death, or at the very least a case of severe bad luck. Where his name

came from or who first decided who the ghost was, no one knows, but it appears that the first reports of the 'floating vicar' were in the 1950s. There is some dispute with regards to the vicar's name even being connected to St Mary's Church, going so far as to claim that Revd Yates never even existed. Some say he is as much of a mystery as the ghost's appear-ance itself.

So, is the story true or false? It is pos-sible that this could be a remake of the story of the floating vicar in Broughton, Flintshire, Wales, where courting cou-ples would often come across the ghost. Back in the 1930s, before the Chester bypass was built, a couple were walking down the Old Warren, a road that led to Buckley, when they suddenly spotted a figure coming towards them. The stranger was very tall and thin, taller than anyone either of them had ever seen before. He was dressed in black, like a vicar, and wore a broad-rimmed hat. The couple then noticed he was not walking but *floating* in the air. As he passed by he never spoke to the couple or even acknowl-

The old grammar school.

St Mary's Church, on Lowgate.

An artist's impression of the grammar school.

edged their presence; this was the case for several more couples who also witnessed the floating vicar. Could someone have come across this tale and brought it to Hull, or is there really a ghost in the grammar school who has been mistaken for a vicar due to his style of dress? Are the witnesses telling the truth? Or has this story been so interesting for so long, people have invented their own experiences for the sake of being able to say that they have indeed seen the floating vicar? Unless you witness him yourself, there is no way of ever knowing if this story garners any truth.

Hull Grammar School was built in 1583, although the school was originally started in 1431, with the first reference to a grammar school in Hull between 1320 and 1347 on Scole Street, before moving to Scole Lane. This was before it was the Grade II Tudor building in Trinity Square. Back then it catered for between forty and fifty boys who were taught by the schoolmaster, who was assisted by an usher. By the 1600s the school taught around 100 boys between the ages of seven and fourteen. Only the ground floor was used by the school as the upper floor was used by the Hull Company of Merchants, until 1706, when they left the building. It was then used as assembly rooms for concerts and dancing up until 1736. Around 1750 it became a private school, boasting William Wilberforce, born 24 August 1759, as one of its former students. William, who had to resign from Parliament in 1825, is best known for his involvement in the abolition of slavery. Even though he was extremely ill, he continued to fight for the Slavery Abolition Act, which was passed in 1833. Seeing the abolishment of slavery in most of the British Empire was a great achievement for him; sadly William died just three days after it was passed.

In the latter part of the nineteenth century, the school building was in a bad state of repair, needing a great deal of restoration, forcing the school to close in 1878. The school was, by then, already in temporary accommodation in Baker Street, whilst waiting for the building of the new school in Leicester Street to be completed – which it was, in 1892. The building in Trinity Square was used for a short period as a warehouse to store potatoes and, in 1883, it was bought by the vicar from Holy Trinity Church to be used as a clergy-house and also as a choir school. Eventually, in 1987, Hull City Council bought the property, which had fallen into disrepair again, and by 1997 the building had become the Hands On History Museum, which offers a great insight into the history of Hull and its people during Victorian times. It also houses an Egyptian Gallery, which includes replica treasures of King Tutankhamun, and a genuine mummy believed to be 2,600 years old. Thankfully

no one has witnessed that walking around, or at least not that I am aware of anyway!

Needing to uncover the mystery surrounding the floating vicar – some claim he exists, others claim he doesn't – I decided to do some research on the matter. After some time, I discovered that there was indeed a Revd Yates in Hull, and although I have not been able to connect him directly to the church or the school, I have managed to trace where he lived. In 1892, a Revd Yates was registered as living at 49 Charlotte Street, which runs from High Street to George Street. Did Revd Yates have any connection to the building on Trinity Square? It is possible that he did during its time as a choir school, as this was during the same period. Even if he was not connected to either St Mary's or Holy Trinity, he may have still rented the room to use with his own choir. I called into the museum to have a look around and whilst there I spoke to two members of staff. One had been working there for a while and had never encountered a ghost, although he did say he had heard strange noises, which were not easily explained by creaking floorboards, and that there was a strange smell of smoke from either a cigarette or cigar that would appear out of the blue. He also relayed his own version of the vicar story to me, claiming that the vicar had fallen down a staircase, the fall breaking his neck and killing him; but this is something that I have been unable to verify. The other member of staff has not any supernatural phenomena at the museum; although it is important to point out that it was in fact her first day working there.

Blue plaque for the Hands On History Museum.

Plaque on the wall of Holy Trinity Church.

I first came across this story in 2007 after receiving an email from a young lady called Sarah, who was in her early twenties, who believed she and a friend had both experienced some strange paranormal happening when they had visited the museum while in the town for the day. Sarah and Karen walked around the building without any concerns until they reached one of the staircases, when Karen felt as if she had slight vertigo at the top of the stairs then a feeling of someone gently pushing her on the back. She grabbed hold of her friend's arm, who guided her down the stairs and out of the building. Once outside, she explained to her friend what had happened, and the strangest thing was that she had an image of a clergyman in her mind as it happened. The two girls thought nothing more of it and decided to go home. Later that night, around 10 p.m., Sarah received a telephone call from Karen's mum to tell her that she had been taken to hospital about an hour before. Concerned and surprised, Sarah asked what had happened, only to hear that Karen had fallen on the stairs, hurting her neck. Sarah rushed to the hospital, only to find her friend being discharged. The doctors had given her the all-clear, saying she was lucky she had not caused more damage to her neck. Sarah asked Karen if she had suffered the vertigo feeling again, to which she replied yes, as well as feeling a hand on her back once again. Sarah looked up the old school on the internet and discovered the story of the ghost of a clergyman, causing her to question whether he could have been the one to push her friend. Neither she nor Karen were aware of the story before and had no idea about the tale of the vicar falling down the staircase breaking his neck.

Another version of the story came from Tony; the retired policeman mentioned in the previous story regarding Hull Prison, who also experienced the ghostly clergyman. It was during the summer months, whilst still serving with the police, that he had his first encounter. He was walking passed the building when he noticed two members of staff leaving and locking the door. He thought nothing of it until he glanced up at the window above and, as he did so, he noticed a dark figure walk by on the inside. Concerned that the staff were about to lock in a visitor, he called out to them, 'I think you have left someone inside, I have just seen someone upstairs.' They quickly pointed out that they had not, as the building had been checked thoroughly before they had left and locked up. Besides, if there was someone

The staircase inside the grammar school, which is now closed off.

to detail, but this figure had no detail to focus my attention on, except that is it wore a long black tunic or something similar.

He then went on to explain that he couldn't describe the face for there wasn't one; it was missing. Tony asked his wife whether she had seen the fgiure, to which she replied she had not, suggesting it may have been a figment of his imagination. The couple went home, the subject closed to all discussion. However, the day after, when Tony visited his uncle and told him about the two incidents, his uncle shared a secret that he had kept to himself for a long time. The uncle had served as an air-raid warden during the Second World War, and whilst on duty he saw a figure in the window dressed in black. On one occasion though it was holding some kind of light, so he shouted up to the figure to turn it out and much to his surprise the figure just faded away in front of his very eyes.

The final two stories regarding the museum relate to incidents that seem to be about prevention, rather than pushing or shoving someone. The first incident comes from a lady called Lesley, who had visited the museum too, although it was some years ago, roughly four or five, she doesn't remember. After walking around the museum, which she found most interesting, she was about to walk down a set of stairs when she lost her balance. But, instead of tripping down the stairs, she felt a hand take hold of her blouse, stopping her from falling and allowing her to regain her balance. Turning around to thank the person, she was amazed

still inside, the alarm would be sounding by now. Thinking that he may have imagined it (after all it was only a quick glimpse), Tony gave no more thought to the incident, until a few weeks later.

Tony and his wife had gone to the museum for a look around. As they neared the window in which Tony thought he had seen the dark figure, he saw it again. This time he was a lot closer to the figure and, in his words,

There was no way I imagined it, I have been on the force for most of my life, you learn to train the eye to attention to find no one nearby who could have helped her. Lesley is convinced it was a helpful, caring ghost that saved her that day. Lesley has since revisited the building in the hope she may experience something else, sadly, she says she has not, except for a strange coldness when she nears the staircase.

The second incident was told to me by Mark Lindsay, whom I mentioned in an earlier part of this book. He told me that his mother went to visit the museum one day and, whilst there, reported on how a pair of unseen hands had stopped her from going down a set of steps in the lower part of the building. Mark was curious and visited the museum himself. With a recording device in his possession, he went around the building to see if he would experience anything as well. It was not until he left that he checked the device, only to discover a voice saying, 'Don't stop following her,' which he claims was said by the voice of a young boy.

These stories raise some confusion, as the first tale tells of Sarah and her friend Karen being pushed down the stairs, yet Lesley and Mark's mum's both seemed to have been prevented from falling. Is the ghost helpful or mischievous? Or did the incident in the first story somehow get misinterpreted by the young ladies? I think this may well be the case. As an investigator of the paranormal, I have often been called to people's homes where they claim there is a malevolent force at work, only to discover that no harm has been caused, although at the time things may have been scary; objects been thrown on the floor, banging of

doors and a sense of anger in a room. It is quite often the case that the ghost does not mean to scare the tenant, but, instead attempting to get their attention, almost like a cry for help, that, once heard, changes the circumstances quite dramatically. If you remember, in Karen's case she had a touch of vertigo, both at the museum and at home. What if, and this is only guesswork, the ghost at the museum was aware she was about to lose her balance and, if she was to fall down the stairs, a serious injury may occur? What if what she described as a gentle push was actually a helping hand reaching out in order to pull her back? However, this does not explain why she felt the hand upon her back at home. But what if she did not feel a hand? It could have been a case of the subconscious mind playing tricks on her; the scenario was almost the same – a staircase and the vertigo –and maybe the two things tricked the mind into believing that the third factor, the hand, was also present even if it was not. If the

The window that looks out towards Trinity Church, through which the floating vicar has been seen.

ghost is a clergyman, surely it would be better explained as an act of concern for the safety of others, not a malevolent act. Indeed, if it had been a sinister act, surely Karen would have felt a shove rather than a gentle touch upon her back.

Never before have I come across a story like this, one that has more twists and turns than a rollercoaster ride at a fairground. I was beginning to think someone else had discovered the same Revd Yates as I had. That they had thought about the timing of the first sightings, the locality of his home to the church and the school, the description of the ghosts and simply assumed it was he, putting all the coincidences together without any research and making the fatal mistake of simply getting it wrong. As the old saying goes, adding two and two together and getting five. If the ghost is real, if it is that of a clergyman and if he is not Revd Yates, then who exactly is he? With the amount of witnesses, there must be some truth about there being a ghost at the building. One more detail to contemplate is, where did the tale in which people would die once they had seen the ghost come from? None of the stories I have come across back up this claim in any way, shape or form. How do we even know people have fallen to their death after seeing him? There is one possible explanation for this version; there may have been two people either together or in the same vicinity, when one of them saw the ghost and muttered with their last breath that they had seen him. If this is so, then where are the witnesses, and, more importantly, where are the reports of those who did die? I guess we will never know the full truth behind this story; it remains, at this moment in time, a mystery.

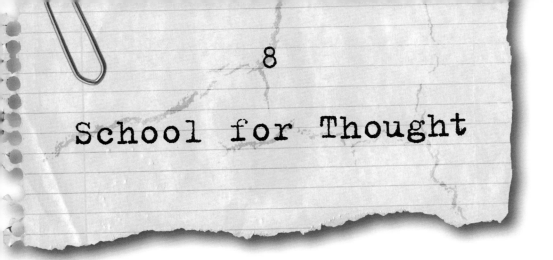

8

School for Thought

IT is not very often that I have to take back something I once said, but in this case that is the exact situation I found myself in. In my previous book, *Haunted Scarborough*, I made the following comment:

It is not very often or usual to come across a story of a school being haunted, but Scarborough can never be accused of shying away from the usual. Most stories that are connected with schools are usually to do with a former teacher or former pupil, who has died tragically with their ghost haunting the place. But sometimes schools are built on the site of another building, and it may be from the former building that the ghost is originally attached to and not the modern school itself.

And yet here I am writing my second book, containing another story about another school that is haunted. The situation is very much the same; this haunting has nothing to do with ghosts of past students or teachers, but people from the building previously on the site – patients and staff from the days a hospital dominated the site. However, even before the hospital was on the site, there had been a workhouse there.

Through research, I discovered that the site was first used as a workhouse that was built between 1843 and 1845, and it was to continue as this for eighty-four years. The building was designed by Henry F. Lockwood, who was also the architect of the nearby workhouse in Hull, along with his partner William Mawson. The workhouse, which is often described as one finest pieces of Victorian gothic architecture, was built along Beverley Road. Today, Beverley Road is just one of several major roads that lead into the city, although it was once one of the most important ways into Hull from the north. The workhouse was believed to be able to accommodate some 500 inmates adequately; however, by 1883, more buildings had been added to the site. Originally known as the Sculcoates workhouse, it changed name at some point to the Beverley Road Institution,

The remains where the Beverley Gate once stood.

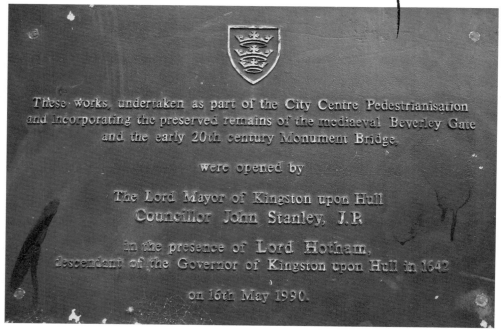

These works, undertaken as part of the City Centre Pedestrianisation
and incorporating the preserved remains of the mediaeval Beverley Gate
and the early 20th century Monument Bridge,

were opened by

The Lord Mayor of Kingston upon Hull
Councillor John Stanley, J.P.

in the presence of Lord Hotham,
descendant of the Governor of Kingston upon Hull in 1642

on 16th May 1990.

The plaque for the Beverley Gate.

before closing in 1929 to become a hospital – the Kingston General Hospital in 1948. In 2002, the buildings were demolished to make way for a school to be erected on the site.

In 1844, a reporter from the *Hull Advertiser* who went to see the original workhouse building during its construction, was so surprised at its splendour that he wrote an article about the site, describing it as having a 'far more noble appearance than any of the fine edifices in that locality' and that it 'would not disgrace the residence of a nobleman', even commenting on how 'the paupers' rooms are spacious, light and airy; and they command a prospect which would be envied by many of our wealthy inhabitants residing in the town'. The reporter then went on to describe the size of the site, explaining how it was 260ft wide and 370ft from front to back. In further detail the reporter explained the purpose and use of each of the areas; the rooms in the centre of the property being used for the Governer and Matron, and on either side of this were the day-rooms which were used by the paupers; there was the kitchen, along with the adjoining dining room, which was situated behind the centre; the paupers bedrooms were above the day-rooms; the remainder of the building housed the schoolrooms, wash-houses, tailors' shops and shoemakers, all found near to the main building. There was also the infirmary, boardroom, clerk's office and waiting rooms, and to the sides of the main building were lodges, for the purpose of receiving the paupers; one for males, the other for females.

During its days as a hospital, staff who worked there said the place was full of strange activity. I first heard about these paranormal happenings in 2004 from a former nurse, who told me that although the hospital had gone and she missed her job, she would not miss the horrible feelings she had felt on several occasions. Claiming to have some psychic ability, she proceeded to tell me that she would often be pestered by tormented souls who seemed trapped between heaven and earth, unable to make the transition into the afterlife. It was often on the nightshift, while there were fewer people around to bear witness to her abilities (and affording her refuge from possible ridicule) that she would help the wondering souls to cross over. There were some souls, however, who were no longer *compos mentis* and were destined to be stuck on the earthly plain for eternity. She could only hope that during the demolition of the hospital, the ghosts would be released to a better place.

While talking to her, she told me of a story that the porters used to scare the nurses with, one that involves apparitions of badly burnt people. It was said that these people died in the National Picture Theatre (which opened in December 1914 on Beverley Road) when it was bombed in the 1941 Blitz. Around 150 people were in the theatre at the time; ironically the picture showing was *The Dictator* starring Charlie Chaplin. However, reports of the time state that despite the building suffering serious damage, no one was seriously hurt.

The former nurse told me that often, during the nightshift, she would find patients talking to people who were not there, when she confronted them, asking

The theatre, originally on Beverley Road, which was bombed during the war.

who they had been talking too, they would say their relatives, who had already passed. Some had even told her their relatives had come to escort them to a better place, paradise, as one patient told her; within hours the patient was dead.

She also told me of a time when her colleague was alerted by an alarm on a monitor going off – the kind which is set off when a patient loses consciousness. The colleague, amongst others, rushed to the bed of the patient, who was an elderly lady. However, as she arrived she saw something that was beyond all comprehension; she could see the patient both on the bed and floating in the air above it. The one floating was almost transparent and was looking down upon the woman

on the bed. The apparition turned her head towards the nurse and smiled, just as the doctor announced that the patient was dead.

It is not unusual for a hospital to be haunted, after all, it is a place where most people end their days on earth. There have been reports all over the country of sightings on wards, in theatre rooms, the morgues and the corridors. In January 2009, one hospital in Derby appeared in a national newspaper, claiming that they had summoned an exorcist after several members of staff had witnessed a ghost wandering the corridors and around the morgue. The newspaper said that managers from the hospital had spoken to the on-site chaplain, who in turn contacted the diocese paranormal adviser to look into the situation, following several reports of a black-cloaked figure being seen. A spokeswoman for the Bishop of Derby said the sightings would be investigated and the necessary appropriate action taken. Some local people believe the ghost is a Roman soldier who died nearby, as the hospital was built on an ancient road constructed by the Romans.

In Hull and Derby the ghosts were deemed to be unthreatening, unlike the one haunting the Northern General Hospital in Sheffield, where, in 2003, two different members of staff reported having the same experience. Both witnesses were asleep in the staff room, when they suddenly awoke to find that an angry matron had placed one hand over their mouths in order to stop them from screaming out, whilst trying to strangle them with the other hand. One of them claimed to have fought off the attacker, only to see her vanish into thin air. However, both witnesses are unable to say whether this was just a dream or whether it was in fact real.

Although I personally have not heard any stories about ghosts on the site since the hospital closed its doors, it would appear that there has been activity taking place since the school has been built. Endeavour High School cost around £15 million to build and claimed to able to hold some 1,200 pupils. According to Mark Lindsay, a paranormal investigator in the town, children at the school claimed to have the seen the ghosts of former patients of the hospital wearing

The entrance to Endeavour School.

white gowns wandering around. Some told their parents that doors would shut even though no one was near them and that the lights would, on occasion, continuously turn on and off without the help of a physical hand. Most of the activity reported to parents by their children would appear to be situated around the area where the hospital morgue would have been. He also informed me that a caretaker was witness to an apparition — a gowned man walking along one of the corridors — and that he even saw it on some footage from the CCTV installed on the site. Sadly, in March 2011, the school appeared in the local paper on several occasions as there had been reports of it having to close down, after a report for the council cabinet stated that the school currently housed around 600 pupils, just half of the capacity it was capable of housing, so therefore making it not financially viable and recommending it for closure. At the time of writing the school is still open, however, its future is uncertain.

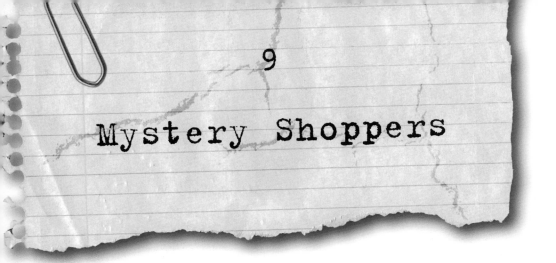

9

Mystery Shoppers

IN 1997, I had an encounter with a ghost which changed my thoughts on the paranormal completely. I was working in a shopping centre in Greater Manchester at the time. One night, whilst carrying out my duties, I was walking around locking up and checking to make sure that no shoppers had been locked in by accident. As I made my way down a stairwell to the rear of the shops, I looked down to see an elderly lady standing at the bottom. I went down to check if she was okay, and engaged in conversation with her. She explained she was on her way for breakfast before going to work, she even gave me her name and address, referring to me as officer as she did, and she also pointed out that she was not trespassing as this was a public footpath. At this point I just assumed she was confused, but agreed with her that she had done no wrong and that I would be more than happy to escort her. That was when I got the surprise of a lifetime; as I started to turn around she dissipated before my very eyes. I had been told several times that the building

had ghosts, but had never taken any of it seriously, and I had never heard stories that mentioned a little old lady. I always assumed the stories had been invented as the building had been built on the site of an old graveyard several years before. Having not lived in the area long, I knew very little about the site's history. Upon doing some research in the local library, I discovered that there once was a footpath that cut through the cemetery, directly where I met the old lady. Digging around a little more, it became apparent that the street the lady had lived on was in direct line of the footpath and a row of local shops. Using the address she had given to me during our brief encounter, I found that she had lived there in the 1950s, the same period that there was a sandwich shop there.

The reason why I have told you this story is because of how closely it links to the following one. The Prospect shopping centre is said to be haunted, just like the centre I used to work in. It was also built on the site where another building used to stand, but this time situated on

The old infirmary, c. 1900.

The Prospect shopping centre.

the site of an old hospital. Hull General Infirmary was built in 1784 and during its construction, which started two years previously, the hospital had temporary accommodation in George Street. The cost of the building was somewhere in the region of £3,000; a mighty sum even by today's standards. When it first opened it comprised of sixty beds, and it operated on a selective basis, unlike the workhouse where you could admit yourself. The infirmary did not allow children, the insane, anyone who was chronically sick, anyone who had fevers, or anyone with skin disorders and venereal diseases. Back then the road was the Beverley turnpike road, which at that time was about a half-mile away from the town as we know it now. This was said to be of benefit to the patients, as it allowed them to breathe in the fresh country air. By 1862 the building needed some alterations, which would continue up until 1939, and was extended to house some 260-plus beds. Due to the air raids during the Second World War the hospital declined somewhat, and, by the time it closed in 1967, it had been reduced to only 150 beds. Eventually, in 1972, the building was demolished to make way for The Prospect shopping centre, which opened in 1974.

One of the hospital's more famous residents was Dr John Alderson, who was born in Lowestoft, Suffolk in 1758. He was elected as physician to Hull General Infirmary when it opened in 1872, before moving to the Prospect Street site in 1784. He was a kind and generous man who gave his services to the hospital for free, and was an honor-

A statue of John Alderson MD, outside the hospital.

ary physician there for an astonishing forty years, whilst also acting as consulting physician to a local Hull charity. He was also well remembered for being the founder of the Sculcoates refuge for the insane, and being a lecturer in physiology. He had some works published, including 'An Essay on the Nature and Origin of the Contagion of Fever'; 'An Essay on the Rhus Toxicodendron, or Sumach, and its Efficacy in Paralysis'; and 'An Essay on Apparitions accounted for independently of Preternatural Agency', which focused on hallucinations experienced by the sick, indicating that the ghosts that some patients claimed to have seen were not real, only illusions. Pretty ironic considering the same building he dedicated so much of his life to is now allegedly haunted.

Since the shopping centre was built, there has been some very strange goings-on taking place in different parts of the building, one of which is in the food court, where utensils and bins have been thrown around by an unseen hand. Even though it no longer serves as a hospital, people claim to have seen the ghosts of nurses wandering around. There have also been stories of people who have heard a baby crying late at night when the shopping centre is closed. A former cleaner informed me that whilst employed at the centre, part of his duties was to clean the male toilets in the food court. On one occasion, when he was alone, he got the distinct feeling that someone was watching him. This also happened to him whilst he was waiting for the service lift, although it was not only that which spooked him, but a door slamming shut behind him too. On two occasions he heard a tap being turned, a toilet flushing whilst the cubicle was empty, as well as the cubicle doors opening and closing on their own. There was also the story of one store manager who watched in complete shock as he witnessed a hook on a display board spinning around.

Although I have not seen this myself, one local remembers that during the grand opening of the shopping centre, a commemorative photograph was taken, and it showed an unidentified person in the line-up; someone who was not present at the time and should not have appeared in the photo. Who was the mysterious figure? No one knows – maybe it was another ghost, perhaps?

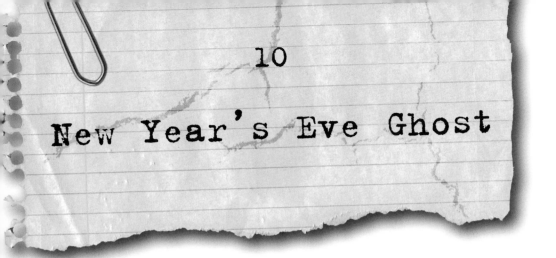

10

New Year's Eve Ghost

WINTER has always been a time for storytelling, ghost storytelling that is. The lead up to Christmas is the best time for these chilling short stories to be told: huddled around the fire in the sitting room, with just a small light on, often a slightly burnt-down candle in the corner, listening to the wind blowing outside the window, the creaking of branchces on a nearby tree, echoing the creaking of the the stairs and floorboards in your home.

When we think of ghost stories around this time of year our thoughts often wander to the famous *A Christmas Carol* by Charles Dickens. The story of Ebenezer Scrooge being visited by the ghost of Jacob Marley, along with the ghosts of Christmas Past, Present and Yet to Come. On this occasion, however, we recall an event that took place one New Year's Eve here in Hull itself.

A group of friends had gathered for an evening of celebration to see out the old year of 1886, by enjoying a meal at the home of Sydney Clarke. After the meal had finished, the group of friends retired to another room to partake in some drinking of port and to enjoy a cigar each. The group had spent a few hours in friendly conversation when one of them suggested they turn their attention to tales of the supernatural. The men decided to each take a turn at storytelling; whether it be a tale they have heard before, or, if possible, a story which involved the speaker himself. Each of the men took turns in sharing their tales of the paranormal, until all but one had spoken. The host of the party, after ensuring they all had another glass of port, began to tell his ghostly tale.

Sydney arose from the comfort of his chair and lent over the lamp, turning it down slightly and making the room more atmospheric for the story he was about to tell. He walked over to the large fireplace, leaning upon it with one arm and holding his glass of port in the other. The start of Sydney's story started in 1880, when he met and fell madly in love with a young lady called Bertha. He approached her father for her hand in marriage, but, unfortunately, her father declined, as Sydney had no fortune to support his daughter and was not worthy of her hand.

Devastated, Sydney left Bertha's home. He had no family who could help him except for one recently widowed uncle, who Sydney lived with. His Uncle Ben had boarded a ship to work on, setting sail for the Americas, and Sydney had not heard from him for a while. Sydney had come to believe his Uncle Ben had left the ship's employment to seek work in America, for this was a place where one's fortune could be made. This sparked an idea in Sydney's mind, that he too would travel to America in search of his fortune. He would then return to Hull and ask once again ask for Bertha's hand in marriage, confident in her father's acceptance the second time around as he would have made his fortune.

Sydney had heard that a passenger ship that was setting sail for New York on 1 January. The ship was taking its voyage at early tide, so Sydney had to be at Albert Dock the night before. It was 11 p.m. and Sydney, accompanied by Bertha, stood at the docks, where they had what must have been a very tearful and emotional goodbye. Bertha left to go home to celebrate the New Year with her family, whilst Sydney waited, dreaming of making his fortune and marrying his beloved sweetheart. Midnight was soon signalled by the tolling of bells from both St Mary's and Holy Trinity. Taking a deep breath and one last look back at his home, picked up his cases and started the ascent up the gangway to board the ship. As he approached the end of the gangway, he could make out the figure of a sailor standing at the end. A strange feeling

come over him, as he had not seen where the figure had appeared from. As he reached the end of the gangway though he recognised the face of the sailor, a face he had not seen for some time, and shouted in an excited voice, 'Uncle Ben! What are you doing here? I thought you were in America!' Suddenly, for no reason at all, an unsettling feeling set in, and before he could ask another question, his uncle stood tall and wide as if to block Sydney's entrance, his arm raised up with his finger pointing back to shore. Sydney knew, although he did not know how, that something was very wrong, that this was his uncle's ghost stopping him from boarding the ship. Sydney turned and at full speed exited the gangway. As he reached the dock he tripped over something, falling and banging his head, rendering him unconscious for a few moments. As he came to he looked out to sea, where he could just make out in the distance the passenger ship he should have been aboard.

Sydney returned home thinking about what had happened. He knew that the person who had stopped him had been an apparition of his uncle, and that his uncle was dead, although he had not heard word of this to confirm it. His thoughts also turned to his beloved Bertha and how he would have to tell her what had happened, but even worse, that he was still in his former position of having little to no finances to approach her father with.

Not long after, he heard that the passenger ship that he should have boarded had become lost, believed to have sunk just off the coast of Cornwall. The last

The dock offices from the 1900s.

sighting of the ship was at the notorious Lizards Point, an area that is known for shipping hazards. This must have been the reason for his Uncle Ben's ghost appearing that night at the end of the gangway; he was there to save the life of his nephew.

Two weeks later, Sydney received a telegram that would shed even more light on that night's events. The telegram informed him that his uncle had indeed died, confirming in Sydney's mind that it was indeed his uncles' ghost he saw that night. On further reading of the telegram he discovered that the day his uncle had died was that very same day, New Year's Eve, and, even more shocking, the time

of death (including the calculated time zone differences) was the exact time he saw the ghost. His uncle was boarding a ship in America only a few split seconds before Sydney had started to walk up the gangway in Hull. However, his uncle had slipped on the wet gangway resulting in his falling between the ship and the dock. It was a rough tide that day and the ship was rocking side to side, which resulted in Ben being crushed between the ship and the harbour wall.

As Sydney was about to discover, this was not the end of the tale. While he mourned the death of his last living relative, he found his luck was about to change

Victoria Pier, c. 1900.

forever. Unbeknownst to Sydney, his uncle had saved a sum of £5,000; a considerable sum today, but in Victorian times an absolute fortune. As there were no other relatives alive, the full amount was inherited by Sydney. He could now approach Bertha's father and once again ask for her hand in marriage, which of course he did, this time with no refusal from her father. The happy sweethearts married, with Sydney investing some of the money into a very successful literary career and buying a home in Hull. The couple never forgot Uncle Ben and his part in their happiness. Every year on New Year's Eve the happy couple would raise a glass, looking up at the night sky, and toast Uncle Ben, their benefactor, before celebrating the New Year – a ritual they would continue for the rest of their lives.

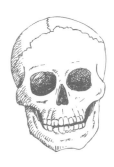

11

The Hull Rapper

DURING the Victorian age, Britain was the world's most powerful nation; a superpower. Often called the *Pax Britannica* period (latin for British peace), it was a time of social inequality, a time for those who had money to enjoy the high society, while the poor lived in squalid conditions in many of the largest towns in the country. Hull suffered as much as London for this.

The then local newspaper of the town, the *Hull Packet*, reported a story on 25 October 1852, about the ghostly goings-on in a house in the town. Describing a ghost that had taken up residence in a secluded house as a marvellous sensation, the newspaper claimed it could be as famous a story as the Cock Lane Ghost in Smithfield London, some ninety years previous.

A family living at 21 Cock Lane, by the famous Smithfield market, were believed to be haunted by a poltergeist. The story became so famous at the time it was told all over the world. It first came to attention in October 1762, when large crowds gathered outside the Kent family home,

with many claiming to have witnessed the strange goings-on first-hand.

William Kent had lost his wife during childbirth and moved from Norfolk into the home in London, and by this time he had taken up with his wife's sister, who also moved with them. They rented the property from a Richard Parsons, who was a parish clerk alleged to have borrowed money from William, who was a usurer (a loan shark) at the time. Due to the strange happenings the family moved out for a short while, but when William won his case against Richard to get his money back they moved back in and, as soon as they did, the strange happenings resumed once again. Fanny, William's eleven-year-old daughter, became a victim of smallpox and passed away, giving Richard the idea to use his own eleven-year-old daughter as a pawn in the saga, claiming that she was also being haunted by the same ghost which resided at the house on Cock Lane. He and his daughter said the ghost was telling her Fanny had been killed by William. Whilst many people believed the story at first,

An artist's impression of Cock Lane, London, from the nineteenth century.

The story based in Hull, however, is about a house on Wellington Lane and its inhabitants – an elderly bedridden lady, her daughter and son-in-law, and their female domestic. The strange occurrences started about a month before the story appeared in the newspaper, when, late one night, the household became disturbed by strange knocking noises on one of the walls; it seemed as though the knocking was being made by a hand none of them could see. At first they all thought nothing of it, until it continued at unusual, irregular times and it seemed to be happening whilst all were present in the room, so each member of the household knew for certain that none of them had been responsible for the actions. The strange knockings continued for four weeks, convincing the family that some supernatural force was at work. One member of the family spoke to the neighbours about the bizarre goings-on, and before they knew it rumours of the 'haunted house' were upon everyone's lips. People from that part of town heard the tale and passed it on to friends and relatives from other parts of the town, spreading the story like wildfire.

The residents of the town became curious as to what the ghost wanted. During Victorian times the paranormal and supernatural gained some momentum, séances were being held in parlours across the country, where mediums would try to commune with the souls of the dead. The dead would often respond to questions by a series of knocking or tapping, and in some cases rapping their unseen hands on the table used during the séance. This is where the term 'spirit

the author Dr Samuel Johnson looked into the claims and found them to be false, causing Elizabeth to confess she had been told by her father to say the things that she did. Richard was found guilty of fraud and pilloried, before serving a two year sentence.

rapping' came from. The people of Hull believed this was taking place in the house on Wellington Lane; a ghost was trying to commune with the residents in order to give some sort of message. One evening, the week before the story appeared in the paper, it was reported by the police that more than a thousand people visited the site to see the home, all waiting to hear the knockings. On 24 October, the reporter claimed that crowds upon crowds of people had gathered again, but they were kept some 100 yards away by police. Despite the weather being extremely cold and damp, the crowds stayed all night, hoping to hear the sounds emanating from the home, and they waited anxiously for the police officers to share with them the time of the last knock.

By now the local constabulary had become concerned about the gathering crowds and the alleged activity in the home, so they stationed two officers in the home to stake-out the sounds. The officers, who had been given the task of finding the answer, also heard the rapping sounds made by the ghostly hand, just as the tenants had claimed. The reporter went on to explain that a portion of the roof had been removed in an attempt to discover some sort of answer, but this helped in no way whatsoever. The police reported that from that morning until midnight, between two and three thousand people had been to the home to witness the sounds for themselves, one officer even said that they would have stayed all through the night if the police had permitted it to continue.

Although the activity continued for a while later, interest soon depleted as the activity lessened, or so people were led to believe. It is claimed that such activity like this does slow down after a couple of weeks, sometimes even a few months. This is known as poltergeist activity. Many believe a real ghost is the cause, whilst others suggest the activity is caused by telekinetic energy from a member of the household. Whatever the cause, the family and those in authority were certainly convinced that something paranormal was taking place.

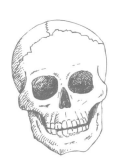

12

More Hull Ghost Stories

Cocoa Mills Ghost

For nearly sixty years there has been a strong smell floating over Hull, coming from The British Cocoa Mills that were once on Tower Street. The site opened sometime in the 1950s and was then taken over in 1997 by an American company called ADM Cocoa, producing cocoa butter and cocoa mass, used by chocolate manufacturers. Sadly, they closed in 2010, an unfortunate time for those employed there, but not for many of the locals who will not miss the smell.

The British Cocoa Mills was rumoured to be haunted and one wonders if the site may still be. The *Hull Daily Mail* reported in May 2011 that I was looking for ghost stories. Since then, I have been told, many times, the following story. Unfortunately, I have been unable to track down the witness to the story, despite being given her first name, so, for the benefit of the story, I have changed her name to Jane.

In 1968, Jane worked at the cocoa mills. She had been enjoying her job until one day, whilst sitting in the can-teen, one of her friends came in. Jane noticed that she looked and sounded very upset, saying, 'I'm leaving here.' She went on to explain that whilst she was working on the conveyor belt, she suddenly felt someone thump her really hard in the back. She turned to see who it was, but there was not a soul in sight. Jane's friend worked alone in that area, so it could not have been a fellow workmate. The experience scared her so much that she was adamant on leaving, which she did, never to return again. Jane soon found herself as her friend's replacement, working on the conveyor belt, only to find that she would have an experience there too. The experience was so profound that Jane even remembers the exact time it took place. It was in the summer on a Wednesday at 3 p.m. when she suddenly felt the temperature drop to almost freezing. She turned her head to the right, only to find herself staring at a headless man of slight build and who stood with a humble posture. At first, for some unknown reason, she felt as though this was someone who

The ADM Cocoa Mills site.

The grounds on which the Cocoa Mills once stood.

knew her, but once the initial shock wore off, she fled from the spot, bringing the whole factory to a complete stop. Jane was sent home sick for two days before returning to work. When she did, she found the manager somewhat reluctant to believe her story. Luckily for her, however, one person did believe her: her forewoman. Taking Jane to one side she told her that she too had seen the headless man. Jane's own daughter-in-law also told her that she had heard of the same apparition being witnessed six years previously, in 1962.

Since the experience Jane has discovered that the apparition had been seen on at least five different occasions, although no one knew who the man was and there seemed to be no mention of an accident on site where someone had been decapitated. She carried on working at the factory for quite a long while, never seeing the headless man again, although she did have one more paranormal experience. It was the same one that her friend had had, and Jane felt as though she had been thumped in the back too. She wondered whether the two were connected, or if there was more than one ghost haunting the mill. This was an answer she would never discover. Due to these experiences, one worker decided to place a cross on the very spot where the headless man had been seen, in hope that this would help the figure to find sanctity. Sadly, I have been unable to find out if this action stopped the appearance or not. Whatever the case, exactly who the headless man is still remains a mystery to this day; or does it? It could be that there is a connection to the following story. It may seem a little farfetched, but there is a chance it holds a possible answer. Read on and draw your own conclusions.

Drowned Parents

For many years the banks of the River Hull have been associated with the story of a drowned couple. Some thought, at first, that they were lovers who took part in a suicide pact. It is only when you hear the ghost story of the Brazil Nut Company that some light is shed on the identity of the couple. The story first came to light in the early 1970s when a female member of staff, who worked as a nut picker, was on her way to the toilet. To get to it she needed to walk down a passage that connected the yard and toilet. As she did so, she looked up to see what appeared to be a grey-haired woman wearing a shawl come through the outside wall. The woman appeared to be dripping wet. The female worker froze on the spot as the lady came near to where she was stood, before she suddenly turned, retraced her steps, and walked back through the wall she had come through. This was strange as there has never been a doorway there, and on the other side of the wall is the bay where barges came along to unload the nuts needed at the mill.

The witness was completely terrified and ran back to her colleagues to tell them what had happened. One concerned friend made her a cup of tea, while another sat with her and explained that she too had witnessed the woman; knowing that someone else had

Above *A lock on the canal where the Brazil Nut Company once stood.*

Below *The canal at the side of the Brazil Nut Company.*

seen it too, and that it was not just her imagination playing tricks on, made the worker feel more at ease. Another colleague who had worked at the mill for a considerable amount of time, asked for a full account of what had just transpired, before giving a possible explanation for the lady's appearance. Many years before, a family tragedy occurred, a tragedy that took four lives. A young boy, aged about six years, and his little sister, aged four, had fallen overboard into the River Hull as they travelled on a barge. Their parents, who saw what happened, ran to the edge and looked into the water to see their two children disappear into the murky water just as another barge was passing in the opposite direction. Fearing that the children would be crushed between the two barges, the parents jumped into the water in a hope to save them. Within seconds, all four had vanished from sight.

Eventually the two children were found by rescuers; the young girl was already dead but her brother was still fighting for his life. They were quickly taken to a room in the mill, where, unfortunately, the young boy died. The man who told this story to his colleagues claims to have seen the two youngsters wandering around the mill, and believes that the dripping lady could be their mother, searching for them. The father, it seems, has never been witnessed. Or has he? Could it be that the father is the headless man from the previous story? His head could have been decapitated by the barges, and his body, which was never found, could have made its way to the cocoa mills, where it is trying in vain to find its family.

Darkman at Debenhams

Debenhams in Hull is the last place you would imagine to be haunted, but one day, whilst listening to the local radio, I heard the presenter talking on the phone to a member of Debenhams staff about the ghost. During their conversation, she mentioned that below the shop there is a room which they call the dungeon. No one likes to go down there, not even the security guards, due to the fact that many of the staff have encountered the ghost of an old man who lurks in the darkness. Some have only felt his presence, while others have seen his shadow wandering around down there. They are not entirely sure who he is or why he is there, but they have come to the conclusion that he worked there in the days when the store was owned by Thornton Varley. The particular area in which he makes himself present is situated where the tailors of the once popular shop used to be, and although the staff have never experienced anything particularly malevolent, they do say the feeling he emits is a threatening one; maybe he doesn't like people entering his space?

Thornton Varley store opened its doors to the people of Hull in 1870. The store was a drapers, then a department store, but sadly the building was bombed during the Second World War, causing the store to be relocated to the Municipal museum, before it too was hit by bombs. They then moved to another location. The original store that had been bombed was taken over by the high street chain Debenhams in 1968. It celebrated its centenary anniversary by planting 100 trees around the town on 15 September 1970 and the comedian Ken Dodd was invited to cut the celebration cake, along with presenting a prize for the Wonder-Bra competition.

I was lucky enough to have a friend. whose Uncle Thomas had been contracted to do some work in the building years ago. I arranged to meet his uncle, who was only too happy to share his story with me. He had worked on the store in the late 1960s or early 1970s and he and a fellow contractor had gone down into the basement. Whilst there, they repeatedly saw a dark shadow moving from the corner of their eyes. Initially they tried to ignore it, but after

Thornton Varley in the 1940s.

about half an hour, the two men could not only hear the sound of their own voices, but what they believed was a third voice. It wasn't talking to them, but was more of a grumbling type of sound, similar to the sound you hear when someone disapproves of all the chit-chat. Maybe it is not only company that the ghost dislikes, just noise in general!

Ghost Train

The Hull Royal Infirmary, as we know it today, was once called the Hull Union Workhouse and was built in 1852. At the time, very little existed nearby, except for the railway building at the level crossing behind the workhouse. It was around 1860 before any other properties were built nearby. The workhouse had originally been the Old Charity Hall on White-Friargate, and dates back to 1698, making it the oldest in the country. It later became the Kingston-upon-Hull Incorporation for the Poor - Poor Law Institution, before becoming the Western General around 1948. It was to the rear of the hospital where the Great Hull Train Crash, as it has come to be known, took place on 14 February 1927. Two trains, the 09.05 Hull to Scarborough and the 08.22 Withernsea to Hull, were travelling in opposite directions when they collided, killing twelve people and injuring forty-six, some of whom were schoolchildren.

Above: The train track where the Great Hull Train Crash occurred.

Left: A Hull rail line signal box, c. 1900.

The extended section of the new hospital.

The old hospital, which is now at the rear of the grounds.

An inquest found that human error was to blame for the crash. At the time there had been three signalmen on duty in the signal box and one of them had pulled the wrong lever by accident. The inquest into the crash found that the man responsible had pulled the lever for the outgoing train rather than for the incoming train. This resulted in the two trains coming face to face and there was nothing the drivers could do to prevent the incident. The plaque outside the hospital in memory of the incident is a replacement one, as the original was stolen some years ago.

I had never heard of the Great Hull Train Crash until a very good friend of mine, Chris, telephoned me one day to tell me that his mum had been taken into hospital. He then proceeded to tell me that she had been placed in the Hull Royal Infirmary, where she had been for a couple of days. After being put on some very strong medication for her illness, she had began to talk gibberish due to the side effects of said medication; or so he thought. She had complained about not being able to get any sleep because of all the noise in the night. He asked her what noise, and she told him there had been a loud bang outside then lots of people running around, screaming and shouting. Next thing, she said, they were knocking a hole in the wall and carrying all these people through and it looked like there had been a nasty accident. Chris was confused and decided to speak to a nurse about the matter, who confirmed that no such thing had happened, but that maybe his mother was seeing apparitions in a re-enactment.

He was still somewhat confused, so asked her to explain. She told him that when the Great Hull Train Crash had happened toward the rear of the hospital, there had been no doors through which they could fetch the wounded, so they had had to knock a hole in a wall in order to bring them through to be treated. Had Chris's mum heard and watched a replay of the whole event? I believe she did, as does my friend Chris, but what do you think?

Knight to Remember

In chapter two I introduced you to the Revd Tom Willis, who told me the story of St Paul's Church. During that interview, he told me about some of the cases he has been involved in whilst working as an exorcist. Although he was unable to give me specific details, he did tell me some short stories and here is one I have added for your pleasure.

Tom's assistance was often called for by the local police force – often the first port of call for people suffering from a haunting but who did not know who to turn to for help. The police would then visit the homes and would contact Tom on the homeowner's behalf, asking him for his help as they were at a loss themselves in these situations. Because of this he had become friendly with one or two of the officers, one of whom was a Chief Inspector. One day, during a conversation the two were having about hauntings, the Inspector revealed to Tom that he lived in a haunted house and things often went bump in the day, never

mind in the night. Due to the strange
goings-on in his house, he could no
longer get a babysitter to watch his children whilst he and his wife went out for
the evening. As soon as they recognised
his voice they said they were too busy
with homework, or had arranged to sit
for someone else.

Tom said he had two daughters who
would be more than happy to babysit
for him. The Inspector asked him if they
would mind, as they may get spooked, to
which Tom replied, 'I am an exorcist, my
children are as used to ghosts as I.' Tom's
teenage daughters, aged 15 and 13 at the
time, agreed, especially when Tom told
them the Inspector had just bought a
brand new Betamax Video player, which
had only just arrived on the market and
were pretty hard to come by. So they
got themselves a movie to take with
them and watch whilst there. Not long
after they had settled down to watch
the movie, however, things started to
happen; bangs and crashes were coming
from upstairs, as well as from the kitchen.
The two girls were not bothered in the
slightest about the noises and continued
to watch the movie. Once it had finished
they went to see if anything had moved,
as they had been told that this is something that can happen. Going into the
kitchen and dining room they noticed
that a picture had fallen to the floor
and that a set of chess pieces, which had
been strategically placed on the board,
had been knocked over. The girls picked
them all up and returned to the living
room to watch another movie, only to
find the telephone was off the hook.

The picture after it had fallen to the floor.

The telephone on the hook.

Little Emily

Tales of past lives are very interesting and I for one have heard many tales regarding such things. The following story was related to me by local man Keith Daddy, who was told it by a colleague at the local further education college. One of their friend's daughters had an incredible imagination, and would often tell them tales of the life she had previous to this one. She claimed to have lived in Hull before, but long ago during Victorian times. Her name then was Emily and she came from a poor working-class family who lived in conditions of squalor. Although her parents would listen intently to the tales she often regaled to them, they tried not to take them too seriously, not at first anyway. That was until one Saturday afternoon, just after the little girl's fourth birthday, when her mother took her into town for a shopping spree. They made their way to Toys 'R' Us, passing Castle Street on the way. On the corner of Castle Street and Commercial Road they would have had to pass the eighteenth-century graveyard, built as an overflow for Hull's Holy Trinity Church.

When they reached the corner of the two roads, the little girl became very agitated suddenly. Her mother took hold of her daughter's hand in order to continue their journey, but the girl started to drag her mother towards the entrance of the graveyard, insisting that they go in. When asked why she wanted to go in there, she replied that she knew this place from her life as Emily, and that she had been buried in the graveyard a long time ago. Her mother was extremely surprised and told her daughter that Emily was not real, that she was just a figment of her imagination. This made no difference to the young girl, who stood by her words, and in an attempt to prove to her daughter that Emily did not exist the mother agreed to go in with her and look at the headstones.

After checking several stones, the daughter dragged her mother towards the rear of the cemetery, where they came across a small stone that stood all alone in a remote part of the cemetery. They approached the stone to discover part of the epitaph was still readable, showing that it was the grave of a young girl who had died at the age of three in 1850-something (the fourth and final digit could not be made out). The rest of the stone was covered in moss, so the mother carefully rubbed it away to discover the hidden inscription of the child's name: Emily.

A headstone on the grave of a child.

The mother was stunned. Were her daughter's dreams real? Or had she seen this grave before? If so, how and when? She herself had never been to this cemetery before, so how could her daughter have? Once home, the mother contacted all her relatives and friends, asking if any of them had visited the graveyard with her daughter, but none had ever been themselves. The girl was far too young to have walked all this way on her own, found the grave, remembered the epitaph and invented a story around what was written. Only one explanation remained; the child had lived a life before this one, the life of poor little Emily.

Missing Heart

We return now to a story told to me by Revd Tom Harris. Even though the tale I am about to tell you happened a long time ago, Tom remembers it well. He recalls that it was late in the evening, a half hour before midnight in fact, when his telephone began to ring. With it being so late, Tom's first thought was that it had to be an emergency. Upon answering the phone he heard what he describes as 'a flustered gentleman's voice'. The man said that both he and his wife had just had a very bizarre experience and felt that they needed the services of the Church. Never one to turn away those in need of help, Tom agreed to visit the couple that very night. After he had finished speaking with the gentleman he immediately set off to see them, and once he arrived at their home, found the couple to be a little shaken and looking somewhat confused.

After calming the couple, he sat down and asked them to tell him what had happened. The husband informed him that they had both been sitting comfortably in their chairs near to the fireplace, listening to records on the stereo. Then, as if from nowhere, a gold chain dropped onto his wife's lap, making her jump slightly. Thinking that her husband had thrown it at her, as they were alone in the house, she called out to him, 'Why did you do that?' This, of course, disturbed the husband from his state of near slumber and he asked her what she was on about, so she told him about the chain on her lap. He pointed out to her that he had not done it; how could he have when he was half asleep? Both were confused as to where the chain had come from and the husband offered the only rational explanation he could, suggesting that it had fallen into her lap from her neck. It was, however, something she disputed, noting that she never wore chains. He then suggestedan alternative theory, that it had fallen from a shelf in the room onto her lap. Once again the wife disputed this, pointing out that there were no shelves in the room for it to have fallen from. After this, they realised they had no plausible explanation for it, and decided to call a man of the cloth.

Tom was as confused as the couple as to how it had happened, so he asked if either of them recognised the chain. They looked at it again and both said yes, the wife told him she had been given it by her granny, but that there had originally been a gold heart-shaped locket on the chain. She had lost the locket and put the chain away for safekeeping, so that she could pair the two together again if she ever found the locket. Tom asked her where she had placed the chain for safe keeping, and she showed him the pot on the fireplace mantel. Looking into the pot, Tom found lots of odd buttons and pins that the wife kept in there, which, she pointed out, the chain had been beneath. Once they had emptied the pot, they discovered that the chain was no longer there, and that the one that had appeared out of nowhere was indeed the chain placed in the pot for safekeeping.

All three of them were now as confused as the next, so Tom asked her if her granny was still alive, to which she told him that sadly she was not — she had passed away the year before. Tom asked whether it had been a full year, or whether it was close to a full year, since she had passed. The couple answered that it was, to which Tom suggested that maybe granny was trying to get their attention. That maybe she wanted the couple to know that she was still with them, and the chain was a way of getting their attention. Suggesting that the three of them say a prayer for granny, he promised to bless the house for them, which he did. Just before leaving he asked the wife, out of curiosity, what had she been doing at the time, to which she told him relaxing and listening to a record she had put on. Tom enquired what the record was, and the lady told him it was 'Take these chains from my heart' by Ray Charles. Tom smiled as he believed the record was appropriate for what had happened, and, upon leaving, promised to return the next day to check on them both.

As promised Tom returned to the couple's home the following afternoon, only to find the couple rather excited as there had been a development in the case. The wife told him that she had been to see her mother that morning, to tell her what had happened to them. After she had relayed the story, her mother offered up another explanation as to why the chain appeared. She had been spring cleaning the night before and had found the locket which belonged to the chain, and that maybe granny was trying to re-unite the two pieces of gold from the other side. They all agreed that granny's ghost had been to both houses, and had given the gift of the locket to her granddaughter once again.

Scott's Warehouse

Between 1979 and 1982, on High Street, Scott's Warehouse was going through some restoration work. Workmen had been in to dismantle some of the machinery there and as they worked they placed their tools, such as spanners and the like, down to the side of them as they went along, so that they would have easy access to them when they were needed.

Nothing unusual occured until the workers went on their tea-breaks. Upon their return, instead of finding their tools in the messy heaps they left them in, they found the tools clean across the other side of the room, arranged neatly in size order. It was as if someone had been in, whilst they were on their break downstairs, to arrange and tidy the area. However, as they all took their break together, it was

The River Hull, behind Scott's warehouse.

deemed impossible for anyone to have snuck off and made their way back in such a short space of time without being noticed. This was no prank, unless there was a playful, yet tidy, ghost present.

This, as the men soon discovered, was not the only ghostly incident to take place.

They soon found out that the warehouse was haunted by another soul. A young lad was stood on a catwalk as he worked on the roof, when he turned to see a man walking towards him. Nothing strange about that you may think, but in this case it was. The young man did not recognise the figure as one of his fellow workmates, and what unnerved him even more was the fact that when he studied the figure closer he noticed that it was wearing very old-fashioned clothing. He went on to say that the man walked right past him and did not even look at him, or acknowledge that he was standing there. The young man left the building and swore never to go back; he never did return.

Not long after the young man's experience, the boss himself had his own encounter with the figure. As he made his way towards the gates, unlocking them in anticipation of the workforce's arrival, he saw a man leaving the warehouse and making his way towards him. Knowing that no one should have been inside at that time, he automatically assumed he was dealing with an intruder. However, when he asked the man who he was, the figure just ignored him, continuing to walk through the now open gates before vanishing into thin air before his eyes. It was not long before people started to talk about these experiences to friends, and another man who had once worked at the site was able to offer an explanation as to who the mystery figure could be. He suggested that the ghost used to be a fitters mate, a job that required the worker to arrange all the tools for the fitter in order of size, neatly in a row. This enabled the fitter to not waste time finding the correct sized spanner, or any other tool, and no time would be wasted tidying them up again once finished. As the story goes, there was once a young man who had worked as a fitters mate who, for some unknown reason, made his way up to the catwalk and hanged himself, and it is this poor soul, so the man suggests, that haunts the old warehouse, tidying as he goes.

Bibliography

BOOKS

Robinson, Peter H., *Third Book of Ghosts and Hauntings,* Hutton Press, 1993

NEWSPAPERS

The Hull Daily Mail

WEBSITES

www.yorkshirehistory.com
www.abbeyghosthunters.co.uk

If you enjoyed this book, you may also be interested in …

Haunted Yorkshire Dales
SUMMER STREVENS

Discover the shadier side of the Dales with this terrifying collection of eerie tales from across the region. Featuring ecclesiastic ectoplasms, ghostly creatures, ladies in black and star-crossed spooks, this book is guaranteed to make your blood run cold. *Haunted Yorkshire Dales* will delight everyone interested in the paranormal.

978 0 7524 5887 8

Yorkshire Villains: Rogues, Rascals and Reprobates
MARGARET DRINKALL

Featuring tales of highwaymen, cut throats, poachers, poisoners, thieves and murderers, all factions of the criminal underworld are included in this remarkable collection of true-life crimes from across the county. Drawing on a wide variety of historical sources and containing many cases which have never before been published, *Yorkshire Villains* will fascinate everyone interested in true crime and the history of Yorkshire.

978 0 7524 6002 4

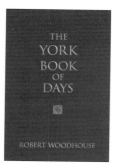

The York Book of Days
ROBERT WOODHOUSE

Taking you through the year day by day, *The York Book of Days* contains a quirky, eccentric, amusing or important event or fact from different periods of history, many of which had a major impact on the religious and political history of England as a whole. Ideal for dipping into, this addictive little book will keep you entertained and informed. Featuring hundreds of snippets of information gleaned from the vaults of York's archives, it will delight residents and visitors alike.

978 0 7524 6045 1

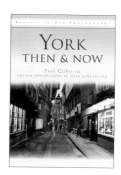

York Then & Now
PAUL CHRYSTAL

As well as delighting the many tourists who visit the city, *York Then & Now* will provide present occupants with a glimpse of how the city used to look, in addition to awakening nostalgic memories for those who used to live or work here. Featuring streets and buildings, shops and businesses, and the people of York, all aspects of life in the city are covered, providing a fascinating insight into the changing face of the city.

978 0 7524 5735 2

Visit our website and discover thousands of other History Press books.
www.thehistorypress.co.uk